ROGER STEVENSON
FEB., 1993

2⁰⁰

Heads

HEADS

Greg Bear

Illustrated by Fred Gambino

St. Martin's Press
New York

Library of Congress Cataloging-in-Publication Data

Bear, Greg.
    Heads / Greg Bear.
       p. cm.
    ISBN 0-312-06367-9
    I. Title.
  PS3552.E157H4   1991
  813″.54—dc20   91-20476
                                                             CIP

First published in Great Britain by Random Century Group.

First U.S. Edition: September 1991
10 9 8 7 6 5 4 3 2 1

For Phil Tippett

HEADS

Order and cold, heat and politics. The imposition of wrong order: anger, death, suicide and destruction. I lost loved ones, lost my illusions and went through mental and physical hell, but what still haunts my dreams, thirty years after, are the great silvery refrigerators four storeys tall hanging motionless in the dark void of the Ice Pit; the force disorder pumps with their constant sucking soundlessness; the dissolving ghost of my sister, Rho; and William Pierce's expression when he faced his lifetime goal, in the Quiet . . .

I believe that Rho and William are dead, but I will never be sure. I am even less sure about the four hundred and ten heads.

Fifty metres beneath the cinereous regolith of Ocean Procellarum, in the geographic centre of the extensive and largely empty Sandoval territories, the Ice Pit was a volcanic burp in the Moon's ancient past, a natural bubble almost ninety metres wide that had once been filled with the aqueous seep of a nearby ice fall.

The Ice Pit had been a lucrative water mine, one of the biggest pure water deposits on the Moon, but it had long since tapped out.

Loath to put family members out of work, my family, the binding multiple of Sandoval, had kept it as a money-losing farm station. It supported three dozen occupants in a space that had once housed three hundred. It was sorely neglected, poorly managed, and worst of all for a lunar establishment, its alleys and warrens were *dirty*. The void itself was empty and unused, its water-conserving atmosphere of nitrogen long since leaked away and its bottom littered with rubble from quakes.

9

In this unlikely place, my brother-in-law William Pierce had proposed seeking absolute zero, the universal ultimate in order, peace and quiet. In asking for the use of the Ice Pit, William had claimed, he would be turning a sow's ear into a scientific silk purse. In return, Sandoval BM would boast a major scientific project, elevating its status within the Triple, and therefore its financial standing. The Ice Pit Station would have a real purpose beyond providing living space for several dozen idle ice miners masquerading as farmers. And William would have something uniquely his own, something truly challenging.

Rho, my sister, supported her husband by using all her considerable energy and charm – and her standing with my grandfather, in whose eyes she could do no wrong.

Despite Grandfather's approval, the idea was subjected to rigorous examination by the Sandoval syndics – the financiers and entrepreneurs, as well as the scientists and engineers, many of whom had worked with William and knew his extraordinary gifts. Rho skilfully navigated his proposal through the maze of scrutiny and criticism.

By a five-four decision of the syndics, with much protest from the financiers and grudging acceptance from the scientists, William's project was approved.

Thomas Sandoval-Rice, the BM's director and chief syndic, gave his own approval reluctantly, but give it he did. He must have seen some use for a high-risk, high-profile research project; times were hard, and prestige could be crucial even for a top-five family.

Thomas decided to use the project as a training ground for promising young family members. Rho spoke up on my behalf, without my knowledge, and I found myself assigned to a position far above what my age and experience deserved: the new station's chief financial manager and requisitions officer.

I was compelled by family loyalties – and the pleas of my sister – to cut loose from formal schooling at the Tranquil and move to the Ice Pit Station. At first I was less than enthusiastic. I felt my calling to be liberal arts rather than

10

finance and management; I had, in family eyes, frittered away my education studying history, philosophy and the terrestrial classics. But I had a fair aptitude for the technical sciences – less aptitude for the theoretical – and had taken a minor in family finances. I felt I could handle the task, if only to show my elders what a liberal mentality could accomplish.

Ostensibly I was in charge of William and his project, answerable to the syndics and financial directors alone; but of course, William quickly established his own pecking order. I was twenty years old at the time; William, thirty-two.

Inside the void, foamed rock was sprayed to insulate and seal in a breathable atmosphere. I oversaw the general clean-up, refitting of already existing warrens and alleys, and investment in a relatively spartan laboratory.

Large refrigerators stored at the station since the end of ice mining were moved into the void, providing far more cooling capacity than William actually needed for his work.

Vibration is heat. The generators that powered the Ice Pit laboratory lay on the surface, their noise and reverberation isolated from the refrigerators and William's equipment and laboratory. What vibration remained was damped by suspension in an intricate network of steel springs and field levitation absorbers.

The Ice Pit's heat radiators also lay near the surface, sunk six metres deep in the shadow of open trenches, never seeing the sun, faces turned towards the all-absorbing blackness of space.

Three years had passed since the conversion. Again and again, William had failed to meet his goal. His demands for equipment had become more extravagant, more expensive, and more often than not, rejected. He had become reclusive, subject to even wider mood swings.

I met William at the beginning of the alley that led to the Ice Pit, in the main lift hollow. We usually saw each other only in passing as he whistled through the cold rock alleys between home and the laboratory. He carried a box of thinker files and two coils of copper tubing and looked comparatively happy.

11

William was a swarthy stick of a man, two metres tall, black eyes deep-set, long narrow chin, lips thin, brows and hair dark as space, with a deep shadow on his jaw. He was seldom calm or quiet, except when working; he could be rude and abrasive. Set loose in a meeting, or conversing on the lunar com net, he sometimes seemed contentious to the point of self-destruction, yet still the people closest to him loved and respected him. Some of the Sandoval engineers considered William a genius with tools and machines, and on those rare occasions when I was privileged to see his musician's hands prodding and persuading, seducing all instrumentality, designing as if by willing consensus of all the material parts, I could only agree; but I loved him much less than I respected him.

In her own idiosyncratic way, Rho was crazy about him; but then, she was just as driven as William. It was a miracle their vectors added.

We matched step. 'Rho's back from Earth. She's flying in from Port Yin,' I said.

'Got her message,' William said, bouncing to touch the rock roof three metres overhead. His glove brought down a few lazy drifts of foamed rock. 'Got to get the arbeiters to spray that.' He used a distracted tone that betrayed no real intent to follow through. 'I've finally straightened out the QL, Micko. The interpreter's making sense. My problems are solved.'

'You always say that before some new effect cuts you down.' We had come to the large, circular, white ceramic door that marked the entrance to the Ice Pit and stopped at the white line that William had crudely painted there, three years ago. The line could be crossed only on his invitation.

The hatch opened. Warm air poured into the corridor; the Ice Pit was always warmer than ambient, being filled with so much equipment. Still, the warm air *smelled* cold; a contradiction I had never been able to resolve.

'I've licked the final source of external radiation,' William said. 'Some terrestrial metal doped with twentieth-century fallout.' He zipped his hand away. 'Replaced it with lunar steel. And the QL is really tied in. I'm getting straight answers out of it – as straight as quantum logic can give. Leave me my illusions.'

'Sorry,' I said. He shrugged magnanimously. 'I'd like to see it in action.'

He stopped, screwed up his face in irritation, then slumped a bit. 'I'm sorry, Mickey. I've been a real wart. You fought for it, you got it for me, you deserve to see it. Come on.'

I followed William over the line and across the forty-metre-long, two-metre-wide wire and girder bridge into the Ice Pit.

William walked ahead of me, between the force disorder pumps. I stopped to look at the ovoid bronze toruses mounted on each side of the bridge. They reminded me of abstract sculptures, and they were among the most sensitive and difficult of William's tools, always active, even when not connected to William's samples.

Passing between the pumps, I felt a twitch in my interior, as if my body were a large ear listening to something it could barely discern: an elusive, sucking silence. William looked back at me and grinned sympathetically. 'Spooky feeling, hm?'

'I hate it,' I said.

'So do I, but it's sweet music, Micko. Sweet music indeed.'

Beyond the pumps and connected to the bridge by a short, narrow walkway, hung the Cavity, enclosed in a steel Faraday cage. Here, within a metre-wide sphere of perfect orbit-fused quartz, the quartz covered with a mirror coating of niobium, were eight thumb-sized ceramic cells, each containing approximately a thousand atoms of copper. Each cell was surrounded by its own superconducting electromagnet. These were the mesoscopic samples, large enough to experience the macroscopic qualities of temperature, small enough to lie within the microscopic realm of quantum forces. They were never allowed to reach a temperature greater than one-millionth Kelvin.

The laboratory lay at the end of the bridge, a hundred square metres of enclosed work space made of thin shaped

13

steel framing covered by black plastic wall. Suspended by vibration-damping cords and springs and field levitation from the high dome of the Ice Pit, three of the four cylindrical refrigerators surrounded the laboratory like the pillars of a tropical temple, overgrown by a jungle of pipes and cables. Waste heat was conveyed through the rubble net at the top of the void and through the foamed rock roof beyond by flexible tubes; the buried radiators on the surface then shed that heat into space.

The fourth and final and largest refrigerator lay directly above the Cavity, sealed to the upper surface of the quartz sphere. From a distance the refrigerator and the Cavity might have resembled a squat, old-fashioned mercury thermometer, with the Cavity serving as bulb.

The T-shaped laboratory had four rooms, two in the neck of the T, one extending on each side to make the wings. William led me through the laboratory door – actually a flexible curtain – into the first room, which was filled with a small metal table and chair, a disassembled nano-works arbeiter, and cabinets of cubes and disks. In the second room, the QL thinker occupied a central platform about half a metre on a side. On the wall to the left of the table were a manual control board – seldom used now – and two windows overlooking the Cavity. The second room was quiet, cool, a bit like a cloister cell.

Almost from the beginning of the project, William had maintained to the syndics – through Rho and myself; we never let him appear in person – that his equipment could not be perfectly tuned by even the most skilled human operators, or by the most complicated of computer controllers. All of his failures, he said in his blackest moods, were due to this problem: the inability of macroscopic controllers to be in sync with the quantum qualities of the samples.

What he – what the *project* – needed was a quantum logic thinker. Yet these were being manufactured only on Earth, and they were not being exported. Because so few were manufactured, the black market of the Triple had none to offer, and the costs of purchasing, avoiding Earth authorities

15

and shipping to the Moon were vast. Rho and I could not convince the syndics to make such a purchase. William had seemed to blame me personally.

Our break came with news of an older-model QL thinker being offered for sale by an Asian industrial consortium. William had determined that this so-called obsolete thinker would suit our needs – it was suspiciously cheap, however, and almost certainly out of date. That didn't bother William.

The syndics had approved this request, to everybody's surprise, I think. It might have been Thomas's final gift and test for William – any more expensive requisitions without at least the prospect of a success and the Ice Pit would be closed.

Rho had gone to Earth to strike a deal with the Asian consortium. The thinker had been packaged, shipped, and had arrived six weeks before. I had not heard from her between the time of the purchase and her message from Port Yin that she had returned to the Moon. She had spent four weeks extra on Earth, and I was more than a little curious to find out what she had been doing there.

William leaned over the platform and patted the QL proudly. 'It's running almost everything now,' he said. 'If we succeed, the QL will take a large share of the credit.'

The QL itself covered perhaps a third of the platform's surface. Beneath the platform lay the QL's separate power supplies; by Triple common law, all thinkers were equipped with supplies capable of lasting a full year without outside replenishment.

'Who'll get the Nobel, you or the QL?' I asked. I bent to the QL's level to peer at its white cylindrical container. William shook his head.

'Nobody off Earth has ever gotten a Nobel, anyway,' he said. 'Surely I get some credit for *telling* the QL about the problem.' I felt the most affection for my brother-in-law when he reacted positively to my acidulous humour.

'What about this?' I asked, touching the interpreter lightly with a finger. Connected to the QL by fist-thick optical cables, covering another half of the platform, the interpreter was a thinker in itself. It addressed the QL's abstruse contemplations and rendered them, as closely as possible, in language humans could understand.

'A marvel all by itself.'

'Tell me about it,' I said.

'You didn't study the files,' William chided.

'I was too busy fighting with the syndics to *study*,' I said. 'Besides, you know theory's never been my greatest strength.'

William knelt behind the opposite side of the table, his expression contemplative, reverent. 'Did you read about Huang-Yi Hsu?'

'Tell me,' I said patiently.

He sighed. 'You paid for it out of ignorance, Mickey. I could have misled you grievously.'

'I trust you, William.'

He accepted that with generous dubiety. 'Huang-Yi Hsu invented post-Boolean three-state logic before 2010. Nobody paid much attention to it until 2030. He was dead by then; had committed suicide rather than submit to Beijing's Rule of Seven. Brilliant man, but I think a true anomaly in human thought. Then a few physicists in the University of Washington's Cramer Lab Group discovered they could put Hsu's work to use solving problems in quantum logic. Post-Boolean and quantum logic were made for each other. By 2060, the first QL thinker had been built, but nobody thought it was successful.

'Fortunately, it was against the law by then to turn off activated thinkers without a court order, but nobody could talk to this one. Its grasp of human languages was inadequate; it couldn't follow their logic. It was a mind in limbo, Mickey; brilliant but totally alien. So it sat in a room at Stanford University's Thinker Development Center for five years before Roger Atkins – you know about Roger Atkins?'

'William,' I warned.

'Before Atkins found the common ground for any functional real logic, the Holy Grail of language and thought . . . his CAL interpreter. Comprehensible All Logics. Which lets

17

us talk to the QL. He died a year later.' William sighed. 'Swan song. So this,' he patted the interpreter, a flat grey box about fifteen centimetres square and nine high, 'lets us talk to *this*.' He patted the QL.

'Why hasn't anybody used a QL as a controller before?' I asked.

'Because even with the interpreter, the QL – *this* QL at any rate – is a monster to work with,' he said. He tapped the display button and a prismatic series of bars and interlacing graphs appeared over the thinker. 'That's why it was so cheap. It has no priorities, no real sense of needs or goals. It thinks, but it may not *solve*. Quantum logic can outline the centre of a problem before it understands the principles and questions, and then, from our point of view, everything ends in confusion. More often than not, it comes up with a solution to a problem not yet stated. It does virtually everything but linear, time's arrow ratiocination. Half of its efforts are meaningless to goal-oriented beings like ourselves, but I can't prune those efforts, because somewhere in them lies the solution to my problems, even if I haven't stated the problem or am not aware that I have a problem. A post-Boolean intelligence. It functions in time and space, yet ignores their restrictions. It's completely in tune with the logic of the Planck-Wheeler continuum, and that's where the solution to my problem lies.'

'So when's your test?'

'Three weeks. Or sooner, if there aren't any more *interruptions*.'

'Am I invited?'

'All doubters, front row seats,' he said. 'Call me when Rho gets in. Tell her I've got it.'

My office lay along a north warren, in an insulated cylindrical chamber that had once been a liquid water tank. It was much larger than I needed, cavernous in fact, and my bed, desk, slate files and other furnishings occupied one small section of about five metres square near the door. I entered, set myself down in a wide air-cushion seat, called up the

Triple Exchange – monetary rates within the Greater Planets economic sphere of Earth, Moon and Mars – and began my daily check on the Sandoval Trust. I could usually gauge the Ice Pit's annual operating expenses by such auguries.

Rho's shuttle landed at Pad Four an hour later. I was engrossed in trust investment performances; she buzzed my line second. William was not answering his.

'Micko, congratulate me! I've got something wonderful,' she said.

'A new terrestrial virus we can't set for,' I said.

'Mickey. This is serious.'

'William says to tell you he's very very close.'

'All right. That's good. Now listen.'

'Where are you?'

'In the personnel lift. *Listen.*'

'Yes.'

'How much extra cooling capacity does William have?'

'You don't know?'

'*Mickey . . .*'

'About eight billion calories. Cold is no problem here. You know that.'

'I have a load of twenty cubic metres coming in. Average density like fatty water, I assume. What would that be, point nine? It's packed in liquid nitrogen at sixty K. Keeping it colder would be much better, especially if we decide on long-term storage . . .'

'What is it? Smuggled nano prochines to liberate lunar industry?'

'You wish. Nothing quite so dangerous. Forty stainless-steel Dewar containers, quite old, vacuum insulated.'

'Anything William would be interested in?'

'I doubt it. Can he spare the extra capacity now?'

'He's never used it before, even when he was close, very close. But he's in no mood for—'

'Meet me at home, then we'll go to the Ice Pit and tell him.'

'You mean ask.'

'I mean *tell*,' Rho said.

The Pierce-Sandoval home was two alleys south of my

office, not far from the farms, off a nice double-width heated mining bore with smooth white walls of foamed rock. I palmed their home doorplate a half-hour later, allowing her time to freshen from the Copernicus trip, never a luxury run.

Rho came out of the bathnook in lunar cotton terry and turban, *zaftig* by lunar standards, shook out her long red hair, and waved a brochure at me as I entered.

'Have you ever heard of the StarTime Preservation Society?' she asked, handing me the ancient glossy folio.

'Paper,' I said, hefting the folio carefully. 'Heavy paper.'

'They had boxes full of these on Earth,' she said. 'Stacked up in a dusty office corner. Leftovers from their platinum time. Have you heard of it?'

'No,' I said, looking through the brochure. Men and women in cold suits; glass tanks filled with mysterious mist; bare rooms blue with cold. A painting of the future as seen from the early twenty-first century; the Moon, oddly enough, glass domes and open-air architecture. *'Resurrection in a time of accomplishment, human maturity and wonder . . .'*

'Corpsicles,' Rho explained when I cast her a blank look.

'Oh,' I said.

'Society capacity of three hundred and seventy; they took in fifty extra before close of term in 2064.'

'Four hundred and twenty bodies?' I asked.

'Heads only. Voluntarily harvested individuals. Each paid half a million terrestrial US dollars. Four hundred and ten survivals, well within the guarantees.'

'You mean, they were *revived*?'

'No,' she said disdainfully. 'Nobody's ever brought back a corpsicle. You know that. Four hundred and ten theoretically revivable. We can't bring them back, but Cailetet BM has complete facilities for brain scan and storage . . .'

'So I've heard – for live individuals.'

She waved that off. 'And doesn't Onnes BM have new solvers for the groups of human mental languages? You study their requests from the central banks, their portfolios. Don't they?'

'I've heard something to that effect.'

20

'If they do, and if we can work a deal between the three BMs, just give me a couple of weeks, and I can read those heads. I can tell you what their memories are, what they were thinking. Without hurting a single frozen neuron. We can do it before anyone on Earth – or anywhere else.'

I looked at her with less than brotherly respect. 'Dust,' I said.

'Flip your own dust, Micko. I'm serious. The heads are coming. I've signed Sandoval to store them.'

'You signed a BM contract?'

'I'm allowed.'

'Who says? Christ, Rho, you haven't talked with anybody—'

'It will be the biggest anthropological coup in lunar history. Four hundred and ten terrestrial heads . . .'

'Dead meat!' I said.

'Expertly stored in deep cold. Minor decay at most.'

'Nobody wants corpiscles, Rho—'

'I had to bid against four other anthropologists, three from Mars and one from the minor planets.'

'Bid?'

'I won,' she said.

'You don't have *that* authority,' I said.

'Yes I do. Under family preservation charter. Look it up. "All family members and legal heirs and – etc., etc. – free hand to make reasonable expenditures to preserve Sandoval records and heritage; to preserve the reputations and fortunes of all established heirs."'

She had lost me. 'What?'

Her look of triumph was carnivorous.

'Robert and Emilia Sandoval,' she said. 'They died on Earth. Remember? They were members of StarTime.'

My jaw dropped. Robert and Emilia Sandoval, our great-grandparents, the first man and woman to make love on the Moon; nine months later, they became the first parents on the Moon, giving birth to our grandmother, Deirdre. In their late middle age, they had returned to Earth, to Oregon in the old United States, leaving their child on the Moon.

21

'They joined the StarTime Preservation Society. Lots of famous people did,' she said.

'So . . . ? I asked, waiting for my astonishment to peak.

'They're in this batch. Guaranteed by the society.'

'Oh, *Rhosalind*,' I said, as if she had just told me someone had died. I felt an incredulous hollow sense of doom. 'They're coming back?'

'Don't worry,' she said. 'Nobody knows but the society trustees and me, and now you.'

'Great-Grandpa and Grandma,' I said.

Rho smiled the kind of smile that had always made me want to hit her. 'Isn't it wonderful?'

William came from an unbound lunar family, the Pierces of Copernicus Research Centre Three. A lunar family even then was not just those born of a single mother and father, but tight associations of sponsored settlers working their way across the lunar surface in new-dug warrens, adding children and living space as they burrowed. Individuals usually kept their own surnames, or added surnames, but claimed allegiance to the central family, even when all the members of the central family had died, as sometimes happened.

As with our own family, the Sandovals, the Pierces were among the original fifteen families established on the Moon in 2019. The Pierces were an odd lot, unofficial histories tell us – aloof and unwilling to pull together with the newer settlers. The original families – called primes – spread out across the Moon, forming and breaking alliances, eventually coming together, under pressure from Earth, into the financial associations later called binding multiples. The Pierces did not bind with any of the nascent multiples, though they formed loose alliances with other families.

The unbound families did not flourish. The Pierces lost influence, despite being primes. Their final disgrace was cooperation with terrestrial governments during the Split, when Earth severed ties with the Moon to punish us for our presumptuous independence. Thereafter, for decades, the Pierces and their kind were social outcasts.

22

By contrast, the allied superfamilies handily survived the crisis.

The Pierces, and most unbound families like them, driven by destitution and resentment, contracted their services in 2094 to the Franco-Polish technological station at Copernicus. They became part of the Copernicus binding multiple of nine families and finally joined the mainstream economy of the post-Split Moon.

Still, the Pierces' descendants faced real prejudice in lunar society. They became known as a wild, churlish lot, and kept to themselves in and around the Copernicus station.

These difficulties had obviously affected William as a child, and made him something of an enigma.

When my sister met William at a Copernicus mixer barn dance, courted him (he was too shy and vulnerable to court her in turn) and finally asked him to join the Sandoval BM as her husband, he had to face the close scrutiny of dozens of dubious family members.

William lacked the almost instinctive urge to unity of a BM-bred child; in an age of rugged individuals tightly fitted into even more rugged and demanding multiples, he was a loner, quick-tempered yet inclined to sentimentality, loyal yet critical, brilliant but prone to choosing tasks so difficult he seemed doomed to always fail.

Yet in those tense months, with Rho's constant coaching, he put on a brilliant performance, adopting a humble and pleasant attitude. He was accepted into the Sandoval Binding Multiple.

Rho was something of a lunar princess. Biologically of the Sandoval line, great-grandchild of Robert and Emilia Sandoval, her future was the concern of far too many, and she developed a closeted attitude of defiance. That she should reach out for the hand of someone like Pierce was both expected, considering her character and upbringing, and shocking.

But old prejudices had softened considerably. Despite the doubts of Rho's very protective 'aunts' and 'uncles', and the strains of initiation and marriage, and despite his occasional reversion to prickly form, William was quickly recognized as a valuable adjunct to our family. He was a brilliant designer and theoretician. For four years he contributed substantially to many of our scientific endeavours, yet adjunct he was, playing a subservient role that must have deeply galled him.

I was fifteen when Rho and William married, and nineteen when he finally broke through this more or less obsequious mask to ask for the Ice Pit. I had never quite understood their attraction for each other; lunar princess drawn to son of out-cast family. But one thing was certain: whatever William did to strain Rho's affections, she could return with interest.

I walked to the Ice Pit with Rho after an hour of helping her prepare her case.

She was absolutely correct; as Sandovals, we had a duty to preserve the reputation and heirs of the Sandoval BM, and even by an advocate's logic, that would include the founders of our core family.

That we were also taking in four hundred and eight outsiders was quite another matter. . . . But as Rho pointed out, the society could hardly sell individuals. Surely nobody would think it a *bad* idea, bringing such a wealth of potential information to the Moon. Tired old Earth didn't want it; just more corpsicles on a world plagued by them. Anonymous heads, harvested in the early twenty-first century, declared dead, stateless, very nearly outside the law, without rights except under the protection of their money and their declining foundation.

The StarTime Preservation Society was actually not *selling* anything or anyone. They were transferring members, chattels and responsibilities to Sandoval BM pending dis-solution of the original society; in short, they were finally, after one hundred and ten years, going cold blue belly up. Bankruptcy was the old term; pernicious exhaustion of means and resources was the new. Well and good; they had guaranteed to their charter members only sixty-one years (inclusive) of tender loving care. After that, they might just as well be out in the warm.

'The societies set up in 2020 and 2030 are declaring exhaustion at the rate of two and three a year now,' Rhosalind said. 'Only one has actually buried dead meat. Most have been bought out by information entrepreneurs and universities.'

'Somebody hopes to make a profit?' I asked.

'Don't be noisy, Micko,' she said, by which she meant incapable of converting information to useful knowledge. 'These aren't just dead people; they're huge libraries. Their memories are theoretically intact; at least, as intact as death and disease allow them to be. There's maybe a five per cent degradation; we can use natural languages algorithms to check and reduce that to maybe three per cent.'

'Very noisy,' I said.

'Nonsense. That's usable recall. Your memories of your seventh birthday have degraded by fifty per cent.'

I tried to remember my seventh birthday; nothing came to mind. 'Why? What happened on my seventh birthday?'

'Not important, Mickey,' Rho said.

'So who wants that sort of information? It's out of date, it's noisy, it's going to be hard to prove provenance . . . much less check it out for accuracy.'

She stopped, brow cloudy, clearly upset. 'You're resisting me on this, aren't you?'

'Rho, I'm in charge of project finances. I *have* to ask dumb questions. What value are these heads to us, even if we can extract information? And' – I held up my hand, about to make a major point – 'what if extraction of information is intrusive? We can't dissect these heads – you've assumed the contracts.'

'I called Cailetet from Tampa, Florida, last week. They say the chance of recovery of neural patterns and states from frozen heads is about eighty per cent, using non-intrusive methods. No nano injections. Lamb shift tweaking. They can pinpoint every molecule in every head from *outside* the containers.'

However outlandish Rho's schemes, she always did a certain amount of planning. I leaned my head to one side and lifted my hands, giving up. 'All right,' I said. 'It's fascinating. The possibilities are—'

'Luminous,' Rho finished for me.

'But who will buy historical information?'

'These are some of the finest minds of the twentieth century,' Rho said. 'We could sell shares in future accomplishments.'

'*If* they're revivable.' We were coming up to the white line and the big porcelain hatch to the Ice Pit. 'They're currently not very active and not very creative,' I commented.

'Do you doubt we'll be able to revive them someday? Maybe in ten or twenty years?'

I shook my head dubiously. 'They talked revival a century ago. High-quality surgical nano wasn't enough to do the trick. You can make a complex machine shine like a gem, fix it up so that everything fits, but if you don't know where to kick it. . . . Long time passing, no eyelids cracking to light of a new day.'

Rho palmed the hatch guard. William took his own sweet time answering. 'I'm an optimist,' she said. 'I always have been.'

'Rho, you've come when I'm busy,' William said over the com.

'Oh, for Christ's sake, William. I'm your wife and I've been gone for three months.' She wasn't irritated; her tone was playfully piqued. The hatch opened, and again I caught the smell of cold in the outrush of warm.

'The heads are ancient,' I said, stepping over the threshold behind her. 'They'll need retraining, re-everything. They're probably elderly, inflexible. . . . But those are hardly major handicaps when you consider that, right now, they're *dead*.'

She shrugged this off and walked briskly across the steel bridge. She'd once told me that William, in his more tense and frustrated moments, enjoyed making love on the bridge. I wondered about harmonics. 'Where's the staff?' she asked.

'William told me to let them go. He said we didn't need them with the QL in control.' We had been working for the past three years with a team of young technicians chosen from several other families around Procellarum. William had informed me two days after the QL's installation that these ten colleagues were no longer needed. He was coldly blunt about it, and he made no dust about the fact that I was the one who would have to arrange for their severance.

His logic was strong; the QL would not need additional human support, and we could use the BM exchange for other purchases. Despite my instincts that this was bad manners between families, I could not stand alone against William; I had served the notices and tried to take or divert the brunt of the anger.

Rho cringed as she sidled between the double toruses of the disorder pumps, whether in reaction to her husband's efficiency or the pumps' effect on her body. She glanced over her shoulder sympathetically. 'Poor Micko.'

William opened the door, threw out his arms in a peremptory fashion, and enfolded Rho.

I love my sister. I do not know whether it was some perverse jealousy or a sincere desire for her well-being that motivated my feeling of unease whenever I saw William embrace her.

'I've got something for us,' Rho said, looking up at him with high-energy, complete-equality adoration.

'Oh,' William said, eyes already wary. 'What?'

I lay in bed, unable to get the noiseless suck of the pumps out of my thoughts, purged from my body. After a restless time I began to slide into my usual lunar doze; made a half-awake comparison between seeing William embrace Rho and feeling the pumps embrace me; thought of William's reaction to Rho's news; smiled a little; slept.

William had not been pleased. An unnecessary intrusion; yes there was excess cooling capacity; yes his arbeiters had the time to construct a secure facility for the heads in the Ice Pit; but he did not need the extra stress now, nor any distractions, because he was *this close* to his goal.

Rho had worked on him with that mix of guileless persuasion and unwavering determination that characterized

27

my sister. I have always equated Rho with the nature-force shakers of history; folks who in their irrational stubbornness shift the course of human rivers, whether for good or ill perhaps not even future generations could decide.

William had given in, of course. It was after all a small distraction, so he finally admitted; the raw materials would come out of the Sandoval BM contingency fund; he might even be able to squeeze in some mutually advantageous equipment denied him for purely fiscal reasons. 'I'll do it mostly for the sake of your honoured ancestors, of course,' William had said.

The heads came by shuttle from Port Yin five days later. Rho and I supervised the deposit at Pad Four, closest to the Ice Pit lift entrance. Packed in cubic steel boxes with their own refrigerators, the heads were slightly bulkier than Rho had estimated. Six cartloads and seven hours after landing, we had them in the equipment lift.

'I've had Nernst BM design an enclosure for William's arbeiters to build,' Rho said. 'These'll keep for another week as is.' She patted the closest box, peering through her helmet with a wide grin.

'You could have chosen someone cheaper,' I groused. Nernst had gained unwarranted status in the past few years; I would have chosen the more reasonable, equally capable Twinning BM.

'Nothing but the best for our progenitors,' Rho said. 'Christ, Mickey. Think about it.' She turned to the boxes mounted in a ring of two crowded stacks in the round lift, small refrigerators sticking from the inward-pointing sides of the boxes. We descended in the shaft. I could not see her face, but I heard the emotion in her voice. 'Think of what it would mean to access them . . .'

I walked around and between the boxes. High-quality, old-fashioned bright steel, beautifully shaped and welded. 'A lot of garrulous old-timers,' I said.

'Mickey.' Her chiding was mild. She knew I was thinking.

'Are they labelled?' I asked.

'That's one problem,' Rho said. 'We have a list of

names, and all the containers are numbered; but StarTime says it can't guarantee a one-to-one match. Records were apparently jumbled after the closing date.'

'How could that happen?' I was shocked by the lack of professionalism more than by the obvious ramifications.

'I don't know.'

'What if StarTime goofed in other ways, and they really *are* just cold meat?' I asked.

Rho shrugged with a casualness that made me cringe, as if, after all her efforts and the expenditure of hard-earned Sandoval capital, such a thing might not be disastrous. 'Then we're out of some money,' she said. 'But I don't think they made that big a goof.'

We slowly pressurized at the bottom of the shaft, Rho watching the containers for any sign of buckling. There was none; they had been expertly packed. 'Nernst BM says it will take two days for William's machines to make this enclosure. Can you supervise? William refuses . . .'

I pulled off my helmet, kicked some surface dust from my boots against a vacuum nozzle, and grinned miserably. 'Sure. I have nothing better to do.'

Rho put her gloved hands on my shoulders. 'Mickey. Brother.'

I looked at the boxes, intrigue growing alarmingly. What if they were alive inside there, and could – in their own deceased way – tell us of their lives? That would be extraordinary; historic. Sandoval BM could gain an enormous amount of publicity, and that would reflect on our net worth in the Triple. 'I'll supervise,' I said. 'But you get Nernst BM to send a human over here and not just an engineering arbeiter. It should be in their design contract; I want someone to personally inspect upon completion.'

'No fear,' Rho said. Gloves removed but skinsuit still on, she gave me a quick hug. 'Let's roll!' She guided the first cartload of stacked boxes through the gate into the Ice Pit storage warren, where they'd be kept for the time being.

*

The first sign of trouble came quickly. Janis Granger, assistant to Fiona Task-Felder, visited barely six hours after the unloading of the heads.

I had neglected to inform Rho about what had happened in lunar politics since her departure to Earth: Fiona Task-Felder's election to president of the Multiple Council, something I would have said was impossible only a year before.

Janis Granger made a meeting request through the Sandoval BM secretary in Port Yin. I okayed the request, though I didn't have the slightest idea what she wanted to talk about. I could hardly refuse to speak with a representative of the council president.

Her private bus landed at Pad Three six hours after I gave permission.

I received her in my spare but spacious formal office in the farm management warrens.

Granger was twenty-seven, black-haired with Eurasian features and Amerindian skin – all tailored. She wore trim flag-blue denims and a white ruffle-necked blouse, the ruffles projecting a changing pattern of delicate white-on-white geometrics. Janis, like her boss and 'sister' Fiona, was a member of Task-Felder BM.

Task-Felder had been founded on Earth as a lunar BM, an unorthodox procedure that had raised eyebrows fifty years before. Membership was allegedly limited to Logologists – nobody knew of any exceptions, at any rate – which made it the only lunar BM founded on religious principles. For these reasons, Task-Felder BM had been outside the loop and comparatively powerless in lunar politics, if such could be called politics: a weave of mutual advantage, politeness, small-community cooperation in the face of clear financial pressures.

The Task-Felder Logologists tended their businesses carefully, played their parts with scrupulous attention to detail and quality, and had carefully distributed favours and loans to other BMs and the council, working their way with incredible speed up the ladder of lunar acceptance,

31

at the same time believing six impossible things before breakfast.

'I have the BM Project Status report from the council,' Janis Granger said, seating herself gracefully in a chair across from mine. I did not sit behind a desk; that was reserved for contract talks or financial dealings. 'I wanted to discuss it with you, since you manage the major scientific project undertaken by Sandoval BM at this time.'

I had heard something about this council report; in its early drafts, it had seemed innocuous, another BM mutual-activity consent agreement.

'We've gotten a consensus of the founding BMs to agree to consult with each other on projects which may affect lunar standing in the Triple,' Granger said.

Why hadn't she gone to the family syndics in Port Yin? Why come all this way to talk with me? 'All right,' I said. 'I assume Sandoval's representative has looked over the agreement.'

'She has. She told me there might be a conflict with a current project, not your primary project. She advised me to send a representative of the president to talk with you; I decided this was important enough I would come myself.'

Granger had an intensity that reminded me of Rho. She did not take her eyes off mine. She did not smile. She leaned forward, elbows still on the chair rests, and said, 'Rhosalind Sandoval has signed a contract to receive terrestrial corpsicles.'

'She has. She's my direct sister, by the way.'

Granger blinked. With any family-oriented BM member, such a comment would have elicited a polite 'Oh, and how is your branch?' She neglected the pleasantry.

'Are you planning resuscitation?' she finally asked.

'No,' I said. *Not as yet.* 'We're speculating on future value.'

'If they're not resuscitated, they have no future value.'

I disagreed with a mild shake of my head. 'That's our worry, nobody else's.'

'The council has expressed concern that your precedent could lead to a flood of corpsicle dumping. The Moon can't

32

possibly receive a hundred thousand dead. It would be a major financial drain.'

'I don't see how a precedent is established,' I said, wondering where she was going to take this.

'Sandoval BM is a major family group. You influence new and offshoot families. We've already had word that two other families are considering similar deals, in case you're on to something. And all of them have contacted Cailetet BM. I believe Rhosalind Sandoval-Pierce has tried to get a formal exclusion contract with Cailetet. Have you approved all this?'

I hadn't; Rho hadn't told me she'd be moving so quickly, but it didn't surprise me. It was a logical step in her scheme. 'I haven't discussed it with her. She has Sandoval priority approval on this project.'

This seemed to take Granger by surprise. 'BM charter priority?'

'Yes.'

'Why?'

I saw no reason to divulge family secrets. If she didn't already know, my instincts told me, she didn't need to know. 'Business privilege, ma'am.'

Granger looked to one side and thought this over for an uncomfortably long time, then returned her eyes to me. 'Cailetet is asking council advice. I've issued a chair statement of disapproval. We think it might adversely effect our currency ratings in the Triple. There are strong moral and religious feelings on Earth now about corpsicles; revival has been outlawed in seven nations. We feel you've been taken advantage of.'

'We don't think so,' I said.

'Nevertheless, the council is considering issuing a re-straining order against any storage or use of the corpsicles.'

'Excuse me,' I said. I reached across to the desk and brought out my manager's slate. 'Auto counsellor, please,' I requested aloud. I keyed in instructions I didn't want Granger to hear, asking for a legal opinion on this possibility. The auto counsellor quickly reported: 'Not legal at this time' and gave citations.

33

'You can't restrain an autonomous chartered BM,' I said. I read out the citations, 'Mutual benefit agreement 35 stroke 2111, reference to charter family agreements, 2102.'

'If sufficient BMs can be convinced of the unwisdom of your actions, and if the financial result could be ruinous to any original charter BM, our council thinker has issued an opinion that you can be restrained.'

It was my turn to pause and think things over.

'Then it seems we might be heading for council debate,' I said.

'I'd regret causing so much fuss,' Granger said. 'Perhaps we can reach an agreement outside of council.'

'Our syndics can discuss it,' I allowed. My backbone was becoming stubbornly stiff. 'But I think it should be openly debated in council.'

She smiled. If, as was alleged by the Logologists, their philosophy removed all human limitations, judging by Janis Granger, I opposed such benefits. There was a control about her that suggested she had nothing to control, neither stray whim nor dangerous passion; automatonous. She chilled me.

'As you wish,' she said. 'This is really not a large matter, It's not worth a lot of trouble.'

Then why bother? 'I agree,' I said. 'I believe the BMs can resolve it among themselves.'

'The council represents the BMs,' Granger said.

I nodded polite agreement. I wanted nothing more than to have her out of my office, out of the Ice Pit Station.

'Thank you for your time,' she said, rising. I escorted her to the lift. She did not say good-bye; merely smiled her unrevealing mannequin smile.

Back in my office, I put through a request for an appointment with Thomas Sandoval-Rice at Port Yin. Then I called Rho and William.

Rho answered. 'Mickey! Cailetet has just accepted our contract.'

That took me back for a second. 'I'm sorry,' I said, confused. 'What?'

34

'What are you sorry about? It's good news. They think they can manage it. They say it's a challenge. They're willing to sign an exclusive.'

'I just had a conversation with Janis Granger.'

'Who's she?'

'Task-Felder. Aide to the president of the council,' I said. 'I think they're going to try to shut us down.'

'Shut down Sandoval BM?' Rho laughed. She thought I was joking.

'No. Shut down your heads project.'

'They can't do that,' she said, still amused.

'Probably not. At any rate, I have a call in to the director.' I was thinking over what Rho had told me. If Cailetet had accepted our contract, then they were either not worried about the council debate, or . . .

Granger had lied to me.

'Mickey, what's this all about?'

'I don't know,' I said. 'I'll field it. The new council president is a Task-Felder. You should keep up on these things, Rho.'

'Who gives a rille? We haven't had any complaints from other BMs. We keep to our boundaries. Task-Felder. Dust them, they're not even a lunar-chartered BM. Aren't they Logologists?'

'They have the talk seat in council,' I said.

'Oh, for the love of,' Rho said. 'They're crazier than mud. When did they get the seat?'

'Two months ago.'

'How did they get it?'

'Careful attention to the social niceties,' I said, tapping my palm with a finger.

Rho considered. 'Did you record your meeting?'

'Of course.' I filed an automatic BM-priority request for Rho and transferred the record to her slate address.

'I'll get back to you, Mickey. Or better yet, come on down to the Ice Pit. William needs someone besides me to talk to, I think. He's having trouble with the QL again, and he's still a little irritated about our heads.'

*

35

My brother-in-law was in a contemplative mood. 'On Earth,' he said, 'in India and Egypt, centuries before they had refrigerators, they had ice, cold drinks, air conditioning. All because they had dry air and clear night skies.'

I sat across the metal table from him in the laboratory's first room. Outside, William's arbeiters were busily, noisily, constructing an enclosure for Rho's heads, using the Nernst BM design. William sat in a tattered metal sling chair, leaving me the guest's cushioned armchair.

'You mean, they used storage batteries or solar power or something,' I said, biting on his nascent anecdote.

He smiled pleasantly, relaxing into the story. 'Nothing so obvious,' he said. 'Pharaoh's servants could have used flat, broad, porous earthenware trays. Filled them with a few centimetres of water, hoping for a particularly dry evening with clear air.'

'Cold air?' I suggested.

'Not particularly important. Egypt was seldom cold. Just dry air and a clear night. *Voilà.* Ice.'

I looked incredulous.

'No kidding,' he said, leaning forward. 'Evaporation and radiation into empty space. Black sky at night; continuous evaporation cooling the tray and the liquid; temperature of the liquid drops; and given almost no humidity, the tray freezes solid. Harvest the ice in the morning, fill the tray again for the next night. Air conditioning, if you had enough surface area, enough trays, and some caves to store the ice.'

'It would have worked?'

'Hell, Micko, it *did* work. Before there was electricity, that's how they made ice. Anyplace dry, with clear night skies . . .'

'Lose a lot of water through evaporation, wouldn't you?'

William shook his head. 'You haven't a gram of romance in you, Micko. Not at all tempted by the thought of a frosty mug of beer for the Pharaoh.'

'Beer,' I said. 'Think of all the beer you could store in Rho's annex.' Beer was a precious commodity in a small lunar station.

He made a face. 'I saw the record of that Granger woman. Is she going to give Rho trouble?'

I shook my head.

'Serves Rho right,' William said. 'Sometimes. . . .' He stood and wiped his face with his hands, then squeezed thumb and pointing finger together, squinting at them. 'You were right. A new problem, Micko, a new *effect*. The QL says the disorder pumps have to be tuned again. It'll take a week. Then we'll hit the zeroth state of matter. Nothing like it since before we were all a twinkle in God's eye.'

We had been through this before. My teasing seemed a necessary anodyne to him when he was bumping against another delay. 'Violation of third law,' I said casually.

He waved that away.

'William, you're an infidel. The third law's a mere bagatelle, like the sound barrier—'

'What if it's more like the speed of light?'

William shut one eye halfway and regarded me balefully. 'You've laid out the money this far. If I'm a fool, you're a worse fool.'

'From your point of view, I wouldn't find that reassuring,' I said, smiling. 'But what do I know. I'm a dry accountant. Set me out under a clear terrestrial night sky and my brain would freeze.'

William laughed. 'You're smarter than you need to be,' he said. 'Violating the third law of thermodynamics – no grief there. It's a sitting duck, Micko. Waiting to be shot.'

'It's been sitting for a long time. Lots of hunters have missed. *You've* missed for three years now.'

'We didn't have quantum logic thinkers and disorder pumps,' William said, staring out into the darkness beyond the small window, face lit orange by flashes of light from the arbeiters at work in the pit below.

'The pumps make me twitch,' I confessed, not for the first time.

William ignored that and turned to me, suddenly solemn. 'If the council tries to stop Rho, you'd better fight them with all you've got. I'm not a Sandoval by birth, Mickey, but by

God, this BM better stand by her.'

'It won't get that far, William,' I said. 'It's all dust. A burble of politics.'

'Tell them to cut the damned politics,' William said softly. The rallying cry of all the Moon's families, all our tightly-bound yet ruggedly individual citizens; how often had I heard that phrase? 'This is Rho's project. If I – if we let her have the Ice Pit for her heads, nobody should interfere. Damn it, that's what the Moon is all about. Do you believe all you hear about the Logologists?'

'I don't know,' I said. 'They certainly don't think like you and me.' I joined William at the window. 'Thank you,' I said.

'For what?'

'For letting Rho do what she wants.'

'She's crazier than I am,' William said with a sigh. 'She says you weren't too pleased at first, either.'

'It's pretty gruesome,' I admitted.

'But you're getting interested?'

'I suppose.'

'The Task-Felder woman made you even more interested?'

I nodded.

William tapped the window's thick glass idly. 'Mickey, Rho has always been protected by Sandoval, by living here on the Moon. The Moon has always encouraged her; free spirit, small population, place for young minds to shine. She's a little naive.'

'We're no different,' I said.

'Perhaps you aren't, but I've seen the rough.'

I leaned my head to one side, giving him that much. 'If by *naive*, you mean she doesn't know what it's like to be in a scrap, you're wrong.'

'She knows intellectually,' William said. 'And she's sharp enough that that may be all she needs. But she doesn't know what a dirty fight really is.'

'You think this is going to get dirty?'

'It doesn't make sense,' William said. 'Four hundred heads is gruesome, but it isn't dangerous, and it's been tolerated on Earth for a century . . .'

'Because nothing ever came of it,' I said. 'And apparently the toleration is wearing thin.'

William rubbed thumb and forefinger along his cheeks, narrowing his already narrow mouth. 'Why would anyone object?'

'For philosophical reasons, maybe,' I said.

William nodded. 'Or religious reasons. Have you read Logologist literature?'

I admitted that I hadn't.

'Neither have I, and I'm sure Rho hasn't. Time we did some research, don't you think?'

I shrugged dubiously, then shivered. 'I don't think I'm going to like what I find.'

William clucked. 'Prejudice, Micko. Pure prejudice. Remember my origins. Maybe the Task-Felders aren't all that forbidding.'

Being accused of prejudgment irritated me. I decided to change the subject and scratch an itch of curiosity. He had shown the QL to me earlier, but had seemed to deliberately avoid demonstrating the thinker. 'Can I talk to it?'

'What?' William asked, then, following my eyes, looked behind him at the table. 'Why not. It's listening to us now. QL, I'd like to introduce my friend and colleague, Mickey Sandoval.'

'Pleased to meet you,' the QL said, its voice gender-neutral, as most thinker voices were. I raised an eyebrow at William. Normal enough, house-trained, almost domestic. He understood my expression of mild disappointment.

'Can you describe Mickey to me?' he asked, feeling challenged now.

'In shape and form it is not unlike yourself,' the thinker said.

'What about his extensions?'

'They differ from yours. Its state is free and dynamic. Its link with you is not primary. Does he want controlling?'

William smiled triumphantly. 'No, QL, he is not an instrumentality. He is like myself.'

'You are instrumentality.'

39

'True, but for convenience's sake only,' William said.

'It thinks you're part of the lab?' I asked.

'Much easier to work with it that way,' William assured me.

'May I ask another question?'

'Be my guest,' William said.

'QL, who's the boss here?'

'If by boss you mean a node of leadership, there is no leader here. The leader will arise at some later date, when the instrumentalities are integrated.'

'When we succeed,' William explained, 'then there will be a boss, a node of leadership; and that will be the successful result itself.'

'You mean, QL thinks that if you achieve absolute zero, that will be the boss?'

William smiled. 'Something like that. Thank you, QL.'

'You're welcome,' the QL replied.

'Not so fast,' I said. 'I have another question.'

William extended his hand, be my guest.

'What do you think will happen if the cells in the Cavity reach absolute zero?'

The interpreter was silent for a moment, and then spoke in a subtly different voice. 'This interpreter is experiencing difficulties translating the QL thinker's response,' it said. 'Do you wish a statement in post-Boolean mathematical symbols by way of direct retinal projection, or the same transferred to a slate address, or an English interpretation?'

'I've already asked this question, of course,' William told me. 'I have the mathematics already, several different versions, several different possibilities.'

'I'd like an English interpretation,' I said.

'Then please be warned that response changes from hour to hour in significant ways,' the interpreter said. 'This might indicate a chaotic wave-mode fluctuation of theory within the QL. In other words, it has not yet formulated an adequate prediction, and cannot. This thinker will present several English-language responses, but warns that they are inadequate for full understanding, which may not be possible for organic human minds at any rate. Do you wish possibly misleading answers?'

'Give us a try,' I said, feeling a sting of resentment. William sat at the manual-control console, willing to let this be my own contest.

'QL postulates that achievement of absolute zero within a significant sample of matter will result in a new state of matter. Since there is a coupling between motion of matter in spacetime and other forces within matter, particularly within atomic nuclei – the principle upon which the force disorder pumps operate – then this new state of matter may be stable, and may require substantial energy input to return to a thermodynamic state. There is a small possibility that this new state may be communicable by quantum forces, and may induce a similar state in closely associated atoms.'

I glanced at William. 'A very small possibility,' William said. 'And I've protected against it. The copper atoms are isolated in a Penning trap and can't come in contact with anything else.'

'Please go on,' I told the interpreter.

'Another possibility involves a hitherto undiscovered coupling between states of spacetime itself and thermo-dynamic motion of matter. If thermodynamism ceases within a sample, the nature of spacetime around the sample may change. Quantum ground states may be affected. Restraints on probabilities of atomic positions may induce an alignment of virtual particle activities, with amplification of other quantum effects, including remote release of quantum information normally communicated between particles and inaccessible to non-communicants.'

'All right,' I said, defeated. 'William, I need an interpreter for your interpreter.'

'What the math says,' William said, eyes shining with what must have been joy or pride, it could not have been sadness, 'is that a kind of crystallization of spacetime will occur.'

'So?'

'Spacetime is naturally amorphous, if we can poetically use terms reserved for matter. Crystallized space would have some interesting properties. Information of quantum states and positions normally communicated only between particles – through the so-called exclusive channels – could be leaked. There could even be propagation of quantum information backwards in time.'

'That doesn't sound good,' I said.

'It would be purely local,' William said. 'Fascinating to study. You could think of it as making space a superconductor of information, rather than the highly limited medium it is now.'

'But is it likely?'

'No,' William said. 'From what I can understand, no QL prediction is likely or unlikely at this point.'

The Ice Pit farms and support warrens occupied some thirty-five hectares and employed ninety family members. That was moderately large for an isolated research facility, but old habits die hard – on the Moon, each station large and small is designed to be autonomous, in case of emergency, natural or political. Stations are more often than not spread so far apart that the habit makes hard sense. Besides, each station must act as an independent social unit, like a village on Earth. The closest major station to us, Port Yin, was six hours away by shuttle.

I had been assigned twelve possible in-family girlfriends at the age of thirteen. Two resided at the Ice Pit. I had met one only casually, but the other, Lucinda Bergman-Sandoval, had been a love friend since we were sixteen. Lucinda worked on the farm that grew the station's food. We saw each other perhaps once a month now, my focus having shifted to extra-family women, as was expected when one approached marriage age. Still, those visits were good times, and we had scheduled a chat dinner date at the farm café this evening.

I've never cared much what women look like. I mean, extraordinary beauty has never impressed me, perhaps because I'm no platinum sheen myself. The Sandoval family had long since accepted pre- and post-birth transforms as a norm, as had most lunar families, and so no son or daughter of Sandoval BM was actively unpleasant to look at. Lucinda's family had given her normal birth, and she had chosen a light transform at age seventeen: she was black-haired, coffee-skinned, purple-eyed, slender and tall, with a long neck and pleasant, wide face. Like most lunar kids, she was bichemical – she could go to Earth or other higher-gravity environments and adjust quickly.

We met in the café, which overlooked the six-hectare farm spread on the surface. Thick field-reinforced windows separated our table from high vacuum; a brass bar circled the enclosure to reassure our instincts that we would not fall off to the regolith or the clear polystone dome below.

Lucinda was a quiet girl, quick and sympathetic. We talked relationships for a while – she was considering an extra-family marriage proposal from a Nernst engineer named Hakim. I had some prospects but was still barn dancing a lot.

'Hakim's willing to be name-second,' she said. 'He's very generous.'

'Wants kids?'

'Of course. He told me they could be ex-utero if I was squeamish.' Lucinda smiled.

'Sounds rad,' I said.

'Oh, he's not. Just . . . generous. I think he's really sweet on me.'

'Advantages?'

She smirked lightly. 'Lots of advantages. His branch controls Nernst Triple contracts.'

'Nernst's done some work for us,' I said.

'Tell,' she instructed me softly.

'I probably shouldn't. I haven't even thought it through . . .'

'Sounds serious.'

'It could be, I suppose. The council president may try to stop something my blood-sister is doing.'

Lucinda raised her wide, thin eyebrows. 'Really? On what grounds?'

'I'm not sure. The president is Task-Felder . . .'

'So?'

'She's a Logologist.'

'Mm hmm. So? They have to play by the rules, too.'

'Of course. I'm not making any accusations . . . But what do you know about Logologists?'

Lucinda thought for a moment. 'They're tough on contracts. Daood – that's Hakim's brother – he administered a design contract to the Independence Station near Fra Mauro. That's a Task-Felder station.'

'I know. I was invited to a barn dance there last month.'

'Did you go?'

I shook my head. 'Too much work.'

'Daood says they rode the Nernst designers for eight weeks, jumped them between three different specs. Seemed to be a management lag – Task-Felder niggles from the top down. No independent thinking from on-site managers. Daood was not impressed.'

I smiled. 'We've upset some Nernst people ourselves. Last year, on the refrigerator repairs and radiator upgrades.'

'Hakim mentioned that . . . Daood said we were saints compared to Task-Felder.'

'Good to know we're appreciated by our brother BMs.'

She mused for a moment. Our food came on an arbeiter delivery cart. 'I've heard about Io, of course. That was hard to believe. Have you read any of Thierry's works?' Lucinda asked. 'They were popular when we were kids.'

'I managed to avoid them,' I said. K. D. Thierry, an Earth-born movie producer who called himself a philosopher and acted like a dictatorial guru, had founded Chromopsychology in the late twentieth century, and then had spun it off into Logology.

'He must have written about three hundred books and LitVids. I read two – *Planetary Spirit* and *Whither Mind?* They were pretty strange. He tried to lay down rules for everything from what to dream to toilet training.'

I laughed. 'Why did you read them?'

Lucinda shrugged. 'I used to scan a lot of LitVids. They were in the library. I called them up, paid the fee – about half

44

what most LitVids cost. Lots of pretty video stuff. Sparkling lakes and rivers on Earth . . . pictures of Thierry riding his solar-powered yacht around the world. That sort of thing. All very attractive to a Moon girl.'

'Did you read anything that explained what happened on Io?'

'I remember something about Thierry being told by an angel that humans were the spawn of warring gods, superbeings. They lived before the birth of our Sun. He said that deep within us were pieces of the personalities of some of these gods.'

'I'll buy that,' I said.

'The rest of the gods' minds had been imprisoned, buried by their enemies under sulphur on the "Hellmoon". They were waiting for us to liberate them and join with them again. Something like that.' She shook her head.

I knew the rest of the story; it was in files on recent history I had studied in secondary. In 2090, Logologists on Mars had taken out a thousand-year development lease on Io from the Triple; violent, useless Io, visited only twice in history by human explorers. The new leaseholders set up a human-occupied station on Io in 2100. The station was lost with all occupants during the formation of a new Pelean-class sulphur lake. Seventy-five loyal Logologists died and were never recovered; they are still there, entombed in black sulphur.

The Logologists had never admitted to looking for lost gods.

I shuddered. 'I didn't know what they were after. That's interesting.'

'It's spooky,' Lucinda said. 'I stopped reading him when I realized he thought he was writing history. These folks think he's practically a god himself.'

'They do?'

'You're dealing with them, and you don't know what they think?'

'My shortcomings are legendary,' I said, raising my hands. 'What kind of god?'

'They say he didn't die, that he was in perfect health. He just left his body behind like a husk. Now he's supposed to advise the Logologists through spiritual messages to his chosen disciples, each generation. He anoints them with blue cold, they say. Whatever that is. So what does Rho want to do that they don't like?'

'My lips are sealed. Rho gives the press conferences around here.'

'But the president knows?'

'I presume she must.'

'Thanks for trusting me, Micko.' She gave me a narrow grin to let me know she was teasing. Still, I felt uncomfortable.

'I can say I don't like any of it,' I confessed. 'It makes things a lot more complicated.'

'Better get on with your homework, then,' she advised.

The deeper I dug into Logology, the more fascinated I became. And repelled – though fascination won out in the end. Here was a creed without a coherent philosophy – a system without a sensible metaphysic. Here was puerile hypothesis and even outright fantasy masquerading as revealed truth. And it was all based on a single supposed insight into the human mind, something so audacious – and so patently ridiculous – that it was fascinating.

K. D. Thierry had exploited everybody's deeply held wish to participate in the unfolding of a Big Event. In this he was little different from other prophets and messiahs; the real differences lay in how much we knew about Thierry, and how ridiculous it seemed that a man such as he could be vouchsafed any great truth.

Thierry had been an actor in his youth. He had played small roles in bad chemstock films, one or two tiny appearances in good ones. He was known to film buffs but not to many others. In time he found his real strength lay in putting together deals, and so he began to produce and even direct films.

By the late 1980s he had made a reputation as the director

of a series of bizarre mystery films in which a peculiar flavour, half lunacy, half ironic humour, attracted a faithful following. He began to lecture at colleges and universities. He allegedly once told a screenwriter in New York that 'Movies are a weak shadow. Religion is where we ought to go.'

And so he went. Not an uneducated man, he joined the chorus then intent on knocking the last crumbling chunks of Freudian doctrine from its pedestal. He tried to add all the rest of psychology to the scraps; his first wife had been a psychotherapist, and the parting had been memorably cruel to both.

Then, when he was forty-three years old, came a night of revelation. Sitting on a beach near the California city of Newport, he was confronted – so he claimed – by a massive figure, tall as a skyscraper, who gave him a piece of rock crystal the size of his fist. The figure was female in shape, but masculine in strength, and it said to him, 'I don't have much time. I've been dead too long to stay here and talk to you in person. This crystal tells the entire story.'

Thierry surmised that the huge figure was a hologram – which seemed to me to be primitive technology for a god to use when manifesting herself, but then, Thierry's imagination was limited by his times, and to reach his presumed audience of scientific naives he used the jargon and concepts of the 1990s.

He stared into the crystal, wrote down what he saw in a series of secret books not published in his lifetime, and then produced an epitome for public consumption. That epitome was called *The Old and the New Human Race*, and in it he revealed the cosmic science of Chromopsychology.

The enormous hologram had been the last of the True Humans, and the crystal she had given him had helped him unlock the power of his mind.

He published and promoted the book personally. It sold ten thousand copies the first year, and five hundred thousand copies the next. Later editions revised the name and some of the doctrines of the cosmic science: it

47

became Logology, his final break with even the word *psychology*.

The Old and the New Human Race was soon available not just in paper, but in cube text, LitVid, Vid and five interactive media.

Through a series of seminars, he converted a few disciples at first, then multitudes, to the belief that humanity had once been godlike in its powers, and was now shackled by ancient chains which made us small, dependent on our bodies, and stupid. Thierry said that all humans were capable of transforming themselves into free-roving, very powerful spirits. The crystal told him how to break these chains through a series of mental exercises, and how to realize that humanity's ancient enemies – all but one, whom he called Shaytana – were dead, powerless to stop our self-liberation. All one's personal liberation required was concentration, education and discipline – and a lifetime membership in the Church of Logology.

Shaytana was Loki and a watered-down Satan combined, too weak to destroy us or even stop strong individuals from breaking free of the chains, wily enough and persistent enough to convince the great majority of humans that death was our destiny and weakness our lot.

Those who opposed Thierry were dupes of Shaytana, or willing cohorts (as Freud, Jung, Adler and all other psychiatrists and psychologists had been). There were many dupes of Shaytana, including presidents, priests, and fellow prophets.

In 1997, Thierry tried to purchase a small South Pacific island to create a community of Unchained. He was rebuffed by the island's inhabitants and forced to move his seedling colony to Idaho, where he started his own small town, Ouranos, named after the progenitor of human consciousness. Ouranos became a major political centre in Idaho; Thierry was in part responsible for the separation of the state into two sections in 2012, the northern calling itself Green Idaho.

He wrote massively, still made movies occasionally. His

later books covered all aspects of a Logologist's life, from pre-natal care to funeral rites and design of grave site. He packaged LitVid on such topics as world economics and politics. Slowly, he became a recluse; by 2031, two years before his death, he saw no one but his mistress and three personal secretaries.

Thierry claimed that a time of crisis would come after his own 'liberation', and that within a century he would return, 'freed of the chains of flesh', to put the Church of Logology into a position of 'temporal power over the nations of the Earth'. 'Our enemies will be cinderized,' he promised, 'and the faithful will see an aeon of spiritual ecstasy.'

At his death, he weighed one hundred and seventy-five kilograms and had to move with the aid of a massive armature, part wheelchair, part robot. Press releases, and reports to his hundreds of thousands of disciples in Ouranos and around the world, described his death as voluntary release. He was accompanying the spirit who had first appeared to him on the beach in California on a tour of the galaxy.

His personal physician – a devoted disciple – claimed that despite his bulk, he was in perfect health, and that his body had changed its internal constitution in such a way as to build up massive amounts of energy necessary to power him in the first few years of his spiritual voyage.

Thierry himself they called the Ascended Master. Allegedly he had made weekly reports to his mistress on his adventures. She lived to a ripe old age, eschewed rejuvenation legal or otherwise, grew massive in bulk and, so the story went, joined her former lover on his pilgrimage.

A year after his death, one of his secretaries was arrested in Green Idaho on charges of child pornography. There was no evidence that Thierry had ever participated in such activities; but the ensuing scandal nearly wrecked the Church of Logology.

The Church recovered with remarkable speed when it sponsored a programme of supporting young LitVid artists. Using the programme as a stepping stone to acceptance among politicians and the general public, Logology's past was soon forgotten, and its current directors – anonymous, efficient and relatively colourless – finished the job that Thierry had begun. They made Logology a legitimate alternative religion, for those who continued to seek such solace.

The Church prospered and made its beginning moves on Puerto Rico. Logologists established a free hospital and 'psychiatric' training centre on the island in 2046, four years before Puerto Rico became the fifty-first state. The island was soon controlled by a solid sixty per cent majority population of Logologists, the greatest concentration of the religion on Earth. Every Puerto Rican representative in the United States Congress since statehood had been a Logologist.

The rest was more or less familiar, including an in-depth history of the Io purchase and expedition.

When I finished poring over the massive amounts of material, I was drained and incredulous. I felt that I understood human nature from a somewhat superior perspective – as someone who was not a Logologist, who had not been taken in by Thierry's falsehoods and fantasies.

I dreamed that night of walking along an irrigation canal in Egypt. Dawn came intensely blue in the east, stars still out overhead. The canal had frozen during the night, which pleased me; it lay in jumbled cubes of ice, clear as glass, and the cubes were rearranging themselves like living things into perfect flat sheets. Order, I thought. *The Pharaoh will be pleased.* But as I looked into the depths of the canal, I saw fish pinned in by the layers of cubes, unable to move, gills flexing frantically, and I realized that I had sinned. I looked up to the stars, blaming them, but they refused to accept responsibility; then I looked to the sides of the canal, among the reeds, and saw copper double toruses on each side, sucking soundlessly. All my dream-muscles twitched and I came awake.

It was eight hundred hours and my personal line was blinking politely. I answered; there were two messages, one from Rho, left three hours earlier, and one from Thomas Sandoval-Rice, an hour after hers.

Rho's message was voice only, and brief. 'Mickey, the director wants to meet with both of us today in Port Yin. He's sending an executive shuttle for us at ten hundred.'

The director's message was extensive text and a vocal from his secretary. 'Mickey, Thomas Sandoval-Rice would like you to meet with him in Port Yin as soon as possible. We'd like Rhosalind to be there as well.' Accompanying the message was text and LitVid on Logology, much of the same material I'd already studied.

I arranged my affairs for the day and cancelled a meeting with family engineers on generator maintenance.

Rho was uncharacteristically sombre as we waited in the Pad Four lounge. Outside, it was lunar night, the brilliant glow of field lights blanking out the stars. Earth was at full above us, a thumbnail-sized spot of bluish light through the overhead ports. All we could see through the lounge windows was a few hectares of ashen churned lunar soil, a pile of rubble dug out from the Ice Pit warrens decades before, the featureless grey concrete of the field itself.

'I feel like they're pushing my nose in the dust,' Rho said. The lights of the executive bus became visible above the horizon. 'This is pretty fancy treatment. The director has never paid us so much attention before.'

I tried to reassure her. 'You've never reeled in Great-Grandma and Grandpa before,' I said.

She shook her head. 'That isn't it. He sent a stack of research on Logologists.'

I nodded. 'Me, too. You've read it?'

'Of course.'

'What did you think?'

'They're odd people, but I can't find anything that would make them object to this project. They say death isn't liberation unless you're enlightened – so frozen heads could just be more potential converts . . .'

'Maybe Thomas knows something more,' I said.

The bus landed, sleek and bright red, an expensive full-pressure, full-cabin late-model Lunar Rover. I had never ridden on the Sandoval limo before. The interior was very impressive; automatic adjustment seats, restaurant unit – I regretted I'd already eaten breakfast, but nibbled on Rho's eggs and mock ham – and complete communications centre. We could have called Earth or Mars or any of the asteroids using Lunar Cooperative statites or even the Triple satellites if we'd wished.

'Makes you realize how far out of the Sandoval mainstream we are at the Ice Pit,' I said as Rho slipped her plate into the return.

'I haven't missed it,' she said. 'We get what we need.'

'William might not agree.'

Rho smiled. 'It's not luxury he's after.'

Port Yin was Procellarum's main interplanetary commerce field and largest city, hub for all the stations in the ocean. Procellarum was the main territory of Sandoval BM, though we had some twenty stations and two smaller ports in the Earthside highlands. Besides being a transportation hub, Port Yin was surrounded by farms; it fed much of the Earthside Moon south and west of the ocean. For lunar citizens, a farm station of sufficient size also acts as a resort – a chance to admire forests and fields.

We passed over the now opaqued rows of farm domes, thousands of hectares spaced along the southeast edge of the port, and came in at the private Sandoval field half an hour before our appointment. That gave us little time to cross by rail and walkway through Yin City's crowds to Centre Port.

The director's secretary led us down the short hall to his small personal office, centrally located among the Sandoval syndic warrens. Thomas Sandoval-Rice was trim, resolutely grey-haired, with a thin nose and ample lips, a middling seventy-five years old, and he wore a formal black suit with red sash and mooncalf slippers. He stood to greet us. There was barely room for three chairs and a desk;

this was his inner sanctum, not the show office for Sandoval clients or other BM reps. Rho looked at me forlornly as we entered; this did indeed seem like the occasion for a dressing-down.

'I'm pleased to see both of you again,' Thomas said as he offered us chairs. 'You're looking well. Mickey, it's been three years, hasn't it, since we approved your position at the Ice Pit?'

'Yes, sir,' I said.

Thomas looked at Rho's wary face and smiled reassurance. 'This is not a visit to a dental mechanic,' he said. 'Rho, I smell a storm coming, and I'd like to have you tell me what kind of storm it might be, and why we're sailing into it.'

'I don't know, sir,' Rho said steadily.

'Mickey?'

'I've read your text, sir. I'm puzzled, as well.'

'The Task-Felder BM is behind all this, everybody's assured me of that. I have friends in the United States of the Western Hemisphere Senate. Friends who are in touch with California Logology, the parent church, as it were. Task-Felder BM is less independent than they want to appear; if California Logology nods its hoary head, Task-Felder jumps. Now, you know that no lunar BM is supposed to operate as either a terrestrial representative or to promote purely religious principles ... That's in the Lunar Binding Multiples Agreements. The constitution of the Moon.'

'Yes, sir,' I said.

'But Task-Felder BM has managed to avoid or ignore a great many of those provisions, and nobody's called them on it, because no BM likes the image of making a council challenge of another fully chartered BM, even one with terrestrial connections. Bad for business, in brief. We all like to think of ourselves as rugged individualists, family first, Moon second, Triple third ... and to hell with the Triple if push comes to shove. Understood?'

'Yes, sir,' I said.

54

'I've served as chief syndic and director of Sandoval BM for twenty-nine years, and in that time, I've seen Task-Felder grow powerful *despite* the distaste of the older, family-based binding multiples. They're sharp, they're quick learners, they have impressive financial backing, and they have a sincerity and a drive that can be disconcerting.'

'I've noticed that, sir,' I said.

Thomas pursed his lips. 'Your conversation with Janis Granger was not pleasant?'

'No, sir.'

'We've done something to offend them, and my sources on Earth tell me they're willing to take off their gloves, get down in the dust and spit up a volcano if they have to. Mud, mud, mud, crazier than.'

'I don't understand why, sir,' Rho said.

'I was hoping one or both of you could enlighten me. You've gone through the brief on their history and beliefs. You don't find anything suggestive?'

'I certainly don't,' Rho said.

'Our frozen Great-Grandma and Great-Grandpa never did anything to upset them?'

'Not that we know of.'

'Rho, we've got some two-facing from our fellow family BMs, haven't we? Nernst and Cailetet are willing to design something for us and take our cash, but they may not stand up for us in the council.' He rubbed his chin for a moment with his finger, making a wry face. 'Is there anybody else interesting in the list of heads, besides Great-Grandma and Great-Grandpa?'

'I've brought along my files, including the list of individuals preserved by StarTime. There's a lacuna I was not aware of, sir – three viable individuals – and I've asked StarTime's advocate in New York for an accounting, but I haven't gotten an answer yet.'

'You've correlated the list?'

'Pardon?' Rho asked.

'You've run cross-checks between Logology connections and the list? In history?'

'No.'

'Mickey?'

'No, sir.'

Thomas glanced at me reproachfully. 'Let me do it now, then,' he said. He took Rho's slate and plugged it into his desktop thinker. With a start, I realized this small green cube was Ellen C, *the* Sandoval thinker, advisor to all the syndics. Ellen C was one of the oldest thinkers on the Moon, somewhat obsolete now, but definitely part of the family. 'Ellen, what do we have here?'

'No interesting strikes or correlations in the first or second degree,' the thinker reported. 'Completed.'

Thomas raised his eyebrows. 'Perhaps a dead end.'

'I'll look into the unnamed three,' Rho said.

'Do that. Now, I'd like to rehearse a few things with you folks. Do you know our weaknesses – your own weaknesses? And the weaknesses of the lunar BM system?'

I could not, in my naivety, come up with any immediate response to this question. Rho was equally blank.

'Allow an older fool to lecture you a bit, then. Grandpa Ian Reiker-Sandoval favoured Rho, doted on her. Gave her anything she wanted. So Rho has the man she wanted, someone from outside who doesn't meet the usual Sandoval criteria for eligible matches. Still, William has done his work admirably, and we all look forward to a breakthrough. However—'

'I'm spoiled,' Rho anticipated him.

'Let's say . . . that you've had a rich girl's leeway, without the corruption of free access to fabulous wealth,' Thomas said. 'Nevertheless, you have substantial BM resources at your disposal, and you have a way of getting us into trouble without really seeing it coming.'

'I'm not sure that's fair,' I said.

'As judgments go, it's extremely fair,' Thomas said, staring at me sharply. 'This is not the first time . . . or are memories short in the younger Sandovals?'

Rho looked up at the ceiling, then at me, then at Thomas. 'The tulips,' she said.

'Sandoval BM lost half a million Triple dollars. Fortunately, we were able to convert the farms to tailored pharmaceuticals. But that was before marriage to William, and it was minor ... although typical of your early adventures. You've matured considerably since then, as I'm sure you'll both agree. Still, Rho has never been caught up in a freefall scuffle. She has always had Sandoval BM firmly behind her. To her credit, she's never brought in the kind of trouble that could reflect badly on the BM. Until now, and I can't pin the blame on her for this, except to say she's not terribly prescient.'

'You blame her for *any* aspect of this?' I asked, still defensive before Thomas's relaxed gaze.

'No,' Thomas said after a pregnant pause. 'I blame you. You, my dear lad, are a focused dilettante, very good in your area, which is the Ice Pit, but not widely experienced. You don't have Rho's ambition, and you haven't shown many signs of her innovative spark ... You've never even taken advantage of your Earth sabbatical. Micko, if I may be familiar, you've done the job of managing the Ice Pit well enough, certainly nothing for us to complain about, but you've had very little experience in the bigger arena of the Triple, and you've grown a little soft sitting out there. You didn't check out Rho's scheme.'

I straightened in my chair. 'It had BM charter—'

'You should *still* have checked it out. You should have smelled something coming. There may be no such thing as prescience, but honed instincts are crucial in our game, Micko.

'You've cultivated fine literature – terrestrial literature – fine music and a little history in the copious time you've had between your bursts of economic activity. You've become something of a lady's man in the barn dances. Fine; you're of an age where such things are natural. But now it's time that you put on some muscle. I'd like you to handle this matter as my accessory. You'll go to the council meetings – one is scheduled in a couple of days – and you'll study up on the chinks in our system's armour.'

I settled back, suddenly more than just uneasy, and not about my impending debut in larger BM politics. 'You think we're approaching a singularity?'

Thomas nodded. 'Whatever your failings, Micko, you are sharp. That's exactly right. A time when all the rules could fail, and all our past oversights come back to haunt us. It's a good possibility. Care to lecture me for a minute?'

I shrugged. 'Sir, I—'

'Stretch your wings, lad. You're not ignorant, else you wouldn't have made that last remark. What singularity faces the BMs now?'

'I can't really say, sir. I don't know which weakness you're referring to, specifically, but—'

'Go on.' Thomas smiled like a genial tiger.

'We've outgrown the lunar constitution. Two million people in fifty-four BMs, that's ten times as many as lived on the Moon when the constitution was written. And actually, it was never written by an individual. It was cobbled together by a committee intent on not stretching or voiding individual BM charters. I think that you think Task-Felder isn't above forcing a constitutional crisis.'

'Yes?'

'If they are planning something like that, now's the time to do it. I've been studying the Triple's performance for the past few years. Lunar BMs have gotten increasingly conservative, sir. Compared with Mars, we've been. . . .'
I was on a nervous high; I waved my hands and smiled placatingly, hoping not to overwhelm or offend.

'Yes?'

'Well, a little like you accuse me of being, sir. Self-contented, taking advantage of the lull. But the Triple is going through a major shake-up now, Earth's economy is suffering its expected forty-year cyclic decline, and the lunar BMs are vulnerable. If we stop cooperating, the Moon could be put into a financial crisis worse than the Split. So everybody's being very cautious, very . . . conservative. The old rough-and-tumble has given way to don't-prick-the-seal.'

'Good,' Thomas said.

'I haven't been a worm, sir,' I said with a pained expression.

'Glad to hear it. And if Task-Felder convinces a significant number of BMs that we're rocking the boat in a way that could lower the lunar rating in the Triple?'

'It could be bad. But why would they do that?' I asked, still puzzled.

Rho picked up my question. 'Tom, how could a few hundred heads bring this on? What's Task-Felder got against us?'

'Nothing at all, dear daughter,' Thomas said. BM elders often referred to family youngsters as if they were their own children. 'That's what worries me most of all.'

Rho returned to the Ice Pit to supervise completion of the chamber for the heads; I stayed behind to prepare for the council meeting. Thomas put me up in Sandoval guest quarters reserved for family, spare but comfortable. I felt depressed, angry with myself for being so vulnerable.

I *hated* disappointing Thomas Sandoval-Rice.

And I took no satisfaction in the thought that perhaps he had stung me to get my blood moving, to spur me to action.

I wanted to avoid any circumstance where he would need to sting me again.

Thomas woke me up from an erratic sleep of one hour, post twelve hours of study. My head felt like a dented air can. 'Tune to general net lunar news,' he said. 'Scroll back the past five minutes.'

I did as he told me and watched the LitVid image.

News of the quarter-hour. Synopsis: Earth questions jurisdiction of Moon in Sandoval BM buy-out of StarTime Preservation Society Contract and transfer of corpsicles.

Expansion 1: The United States Congressional Office of Triple Relations has issued an advisory alliance alert to the Lunar Council of

Binding Multiples that Sandoval BM purchase of preservation contracts of four hundred and ten frozen heads of deceased twenty-first-century individuals may be invalid, under a late twentieth-century law regarding retention of archaeological artifacts within cultural and national boundaries. StarTime Preservation Society, a deceased-estate financed partnership group now dissolved on Earth, has already transferred 'members, chattels, and responsibilities' to Sandoval BM. Sandoval Chief Syndic Thomas Sandoval-Rice states that the heads are legally under control of his binding multiple, subject to . . .

The report continued in that vein for eight thousand words of text and four minutes of recorded interviews. It concluded with a kicker, an interview with Puerto Rican Senator Pauline Grandville: *'If the Moon can simply ignore the feelings and desires of its terrestrial forebears, then that could call into question the entire matrix of Earth-Moon relations.'*

I transferred to Thomas's line. 'It's amazing,' I said.

'Not at all,' Thomas said. 'I've run a search of the Earth-Moon LitVids and terrestrial press. It's in your hopper now.'

'I've been reading all night, sir—'

Thomas glared at me. 'I wouldn't have expected any less. We don't have much time.'

'Sir, I'd be able to pinpoint my research if you'd let me know your strategy, your plan of battle.'

'I don't have one yet, Micko. And neither should you. These are just the opening rounds. Never fire your guns before you've chosen a target.'

'Did you know about this earlier? That California would tell Puerto Rico to do something like this?'

'I had a hint, nothing more. But my sources are quiet now. No more tattling from Earth, I'm afraid. We're on our own.'

I wanted to ask him why the sources were quiet, but I sensed I'd used up my ration of questions.

Never in my life had I faced a problem with interplanetary implications. I finished a full eighteen hours of research, hardly more enlightened than when I had started, though

I was full of facts: facts about Task-Felder, facts about the council president and her aide, yet more facts about Logology.

I was depressed and angry. I sat head in hands for fully an hour, wondering why the world was picking on me. At least I had a partial answer to Thomas's criticisms – short of actual precognition, I didn't think anybody could have intuited such an outcome to Rho's venture.

I lifted my head to answer a private-line call, routed to the guest quarters.

'I have a live call direct from Port Yin for Mr Mickey Sandoval.'

'That's me,' I said.

The secretary connected and the face of Fiona Task-Felder, president of the council, clicked into vid. 'Mr Sandoval, may I speak to you for a few minutes?'

I was stunned. 'I'm sorry, I wasn't expecting . . . a call. Not here.'

'I like to work direct, especially when my underlings screw up, as I trust Janis did.'

'Uh . . .'

'Do you have a few minutes?'

'Please, Madam President . . . I'd much rather hold this conversation with our chief syndic tied in . . .'

'I'd rather not, Mr Sandoval. Just a few questions, and maybe we can patch all this up.'

Fiona Task-Felder could hardly have looked more different from her aide. She was grey-haired, in her late sixties, with a muscular build that showed hours of careful exercise. She wore stretch casuals beneath her short council collar and seal. She looked vigorous and friendly and motherly, and was a handsome woman, but in a natural way, quite the reverse of Granger's studied, artificial hardness.

I should have known better, but I said, 'All right. I'll try to answer as best I can . . .'

'Why does your sister want these heads?' the president asked.

'We've already explained that.'

61

'Not to anybody's satisfaction but your own, perhaps. I've learned that your grandparents – pardon me, your great-grandparents – are among them. Is that your sole reason?'

'I don't think now's the time to discuss this, not without my sister being available, and certainly not without our director.'

'I'm trying hard to understand, Mr Sandoval. I think we should meet casually, without any interference from aides and syndics, and straighten this out quickly, before somebody else screws it up out of all proportion. Is that possible?'

'I think Rho could explain—'

'Fine, then bring her.'

'I'm sorry, but—'

She gave me a motherly expression of irritation, as if with a wayward son – or irritating lover. 'I'm giving you a rare opportunity. In the old lunar spirit of one-on-one, and cut the politics. I think we can work it out. If we work fast.'

I felt way out of my depth. I was being asked to step outside of formal procedures . . . to make a decision immediately.

I knew the only way to play *that* game was to ignore her unexpressed rules.

'All right,' I said.

'I have an appointment available on the third at ten hundred. Is that acceptable?'

That was three days away. I calculated quickly; I'd be back in the Ice Pit Station by then, and that meant I'd have to hire a special shuttle flight. 'I'll be there,' I said.

'I'm looking forward to it,' Task-Felder said, and left me alone in the guest room to think out my options.

I did not break the unexpressed rules of her game. I did not talk to Thomas Sandoval-Rice. Nor did I tell Rho what I was doing. Before leaving Port Yin for a return trip to the Ice Pit, I secretly booked a non-scheduled round-trip shuttle, spending a great deal of Sandoval money on one passenger; thankfully, because of my position at the station, I did not have to give details.

I doubted that Thomas or Rho would look for me during the time I was gone; six hours going, a few hours there, and six back. I could leave custom messages for whoever might call, including Rho or Thomas or – much less likely – William.

To this day I experience a sick twist in my stomach when I ask myself why I did not follow through with my original thought, and tell Thomas about the president's call. I think perhaps it was youthful ego, wounded by Thomas's dressing-down; ego plus a strange gratification that the council *president* was going to see me personally, to put aside a block of her time to speak to someone not even an assistant syndic. Me. To speak to *me*.

I knew I was not doing what I should be doing, but like a mouse entranced by a snake, I ignored them all – a tendency of behaviour I have since learned I was not unique in possessing. A tendency common in some lunar citizens.

We habitually cry out, 'Cut the politics.' But the challenge and intrigue of politics seduces us every time.

I honestly thought I could beat out Fiona Task-Felder.

As our arbeiters executed the Nernst design, the repository for the heads resembled a flattened doughnut lying on its side, a wide circular passageway with heads stored in seven tiers of cubicles around the outer perimeter. It would lie neatly in the bottom cup of the void, seven metres below the laboratory, out of range of whatever peculiar fluctuations might occur in the force disorder pumps during William's tests, and easily connected to the refrigerators. Lunar rock would insulate the outer torus; pipes and other fittings could be neatly dropped from the refrigerators above. A small elevator from the side of the bridge opposite the Cavity would give access.

It was a neat design, as we expected from Nernst BM. Our arbeiters performed flawlessly, although they were ten years out of date.

Not once did anyone mention problems with the council. I started to feel cocky; the plans I'd had of talking to Thomas

about the visit with the president faded in and out with my mood. I could handle her; the threat was minimal. If I was sufficiently cagey, I could drop right in, leap right out, no harm although perhaps no benefits, either.

The day after I finished oversight and inspection on the chamber, and received a Nernst designer's inspection report, and after the last of Rho's heads had been installed in their cubicles, I stamped my approval for final payment to Nernst, called in the Cailetet consultants to look over the facilities, packed my travel bag, and was off.

There is a grey sameness to a lunar ocean's surface that induces a state of hypnosis, a mix of fascination at the lifeless expanse, never quite encompassed by memory, and incredible boredom. Parts of the Moon are beautiful in a rugged way, even to a citizen. Crater walls, rilled terrain, even the painted flats of ancient vents.

Life on the Moon is a process of turning inwards, towards interior living spaces, towards an interior you. Lunar citizens are exceptional at introspection and decoration and indoor arts and crafts. Some of the finest craftsmen and artists in the solar system reside on the Moon; their work commands high prices throughout the Triple.

Two hours into the journey, I fell asleep and dreamed of Egypt again, endless dry deserts beyond the thin green belts of the Nile, deserts populated by mummies leading camels. Camels carrying trays of ice, making sounds like force disorder pumps . . .

I awoke quickly and cursed William for that story, for its peculiar fascination. What was so strange about space sucking heat from trays of water? That was the principle behind our own heat exchangers on the surface above the Ice Pit. Still, I could not conceive of a sky on Earth as black as the Moon's, as all-forgiving, all-absorbing.

The shuttle made a smooth landing minutes later at Port Yin, and I disembarked, part of me still believing I would go to Thomas's office first, an hour before my appointment.

I did not. I spent that hour shopping for a birthday present for a girl in Copernicus Station. A girl I was not particularly courting at the time; something to pass an hour. My mind was blank.

I walked and took the skids, using the time to prepare myself. I was not stupid enough to believe there was no danger; I even felt with one part of my mind that what I was doing was more likely to turn out badly than otherwise. But I skidded along towards the council president's offices regardless, and in my defence I must say that my self-assurance still overcame my doubts. On the average, I felt more confident than ill-at-ease.

It was politics. My entire upbringing had ingrained in me the essential triviality of lunar politics. Council officers were merely secretaries to a bunch of congenial family businesses, dotting the 'i's and crossing the 't's of rules of cooperation that probably would have been followed anyway, out of simple courtesy and for the sake of mutual benefit.

Most of our ancestors had been engineers and miners exported from the Earth; conservative and independent, suspicious of any authority, strongly convinced that large groups of people could live in comparative peace and prosperity without layers of government and bureaucracy.

My ancestors worked to squash the natural growth of such layers: 'Cut the politics' was their constant cry, followed by shaking heads and raised eyes. Political organization was evil, representative government an imposition. Why have a representative when you could interact personally? Keep it small, direct and uncomplicated, they believed, and freedom would necessarily follow.

They couldn't keep it small. The Moon had already grown to such a point that layers of government and representation were necessary. But as with sexual attitudes in some Earth cultures, necessity was no guarantee of responsibility and planning.

From the beginning, our prime families and founders – including, I must say, Emilia and Robert – had screwed up the lunar constitution, if the patched-up collations of hearsay and station charters could even be called such.

When complex organization did come, it was haphazard, unenthusiastically organic, undisciplined. When the Split broke our economic supply lines with Earth, and when the first binding multiples came, the Moon was a reservoir of naively amenable suckers, but blessedly lucky – at first. The binding multiples weren't political organizations – they were business families, extensions of individuals, the Lunars said. Lunar citizens saw nothing wrong with family structures or even syndicates; they saw nothing wrong with the complex structures of the binding multiples, because somehow they did not qualify as government.

When the binding multiples had to set up offices to work with each other, and share legal codes written and unwritten to prevent friction, that was not government; it was pragmatism. And when the binding multiples formed a council, why, that was nothing more sinister than business folks getting together to talk and achieve individual consensus. (That oxymoron – individual consensus – was actually common then.) The Council of Binding Multiples was nothing more than a committee organized to reduce frictions between the business syndicates – at first. It was decorative and weak.

We were still innocent and did not know that the price of freedom – of individuality – is attention to politics, careful planning, careful organization; philosophy is no more a barrier against political disaster than it is against plague.

Think me naive; I was. We all were.

The offices of the council president were located in the council annex to Port Yin's western domicile district; in the suburbs, as it were, and away from the centre of BM activity, as befitted a political institution. The offices were numerous but not sumptuous; the syndics of many small BMs could have displayed more opulence.

I entered the reception area, a cubicle barely four metres square, with a man behind a desk to supplement an automated appointments system.

'Good day,' the man said. He was perhaps fifty, grey-haired, blunt-nosed, with a pleasant but discriminating expression.

'Mickey Sandoval,' I said. 'I have an invitation from the president.'

'Indeed you do, Mr Sandoval. You're about three minutes early, but I believe the president is free now.' The automated appointments clerk produced a screenful of information. 'Yes, Mr Sandoval. Please go in.' He gestured towards a double door on his left, which opened to a long hallway. 'At the end. Ignore the mess, please; the administration is still moving in.'

Boxes of information cubes and other files lined the hallway in neat stacks. Several young women in Port Yin drabs – a style I did not find attractive – were moving files into an office along the hallway by electric cart. They smiled at me as I passed. I returned their smiles.

I was full of confidence, walking into the attractive, the seductive and yet trivial inner sanctum. These were all doubtless Logologists. The council presidents could choose all staff members from their own BM if they so desired. There would never be any accusations of nepotism or favouritism in a political climate where such was the expected, the norm.

Fiona Task-Felder's office was at the end of the hall. Wide lunar oak doors opened automatically as I approached, and the president herself stepped forward to shake my hand.

'Thanks for shuttling in,' she said. 'Mr Sandoval—'

'Mickey, please,' I said.

'Fiona to you, as well. We're just getting settled here. Come sit; let's talk and see if some sort of accommodation can be reached between the council and Sandoval.'

Subtly, she had just informed me that Sandoval was on the outs, that we somehow stood apart from our fellow BMs. I did not bristle at the suggestion. I noted it, but assumed it was unintentional. Lunar politics was almost unfailingly polite, and this seemed too abrupt.

68

'Fruit juice? That's all we're serving here,' Fiona said with a smile. She was even more fit-looking in person, solid and square-shouldered, hair strong and stiff and cut short, eyes clear blue and surrounded by fine wrinkles, what my mother had once called 'time's dividends'. I took a glass of apple juice and sat at one end of the broad curved desk, where two screens and two keyboards waited.

'I understand the installation is already made, and that Cailetet is beginning its work now,' the president said.

I nodded.

'How far along?' she asked.

'Not very,' I said.

'Have you revived any heads?'

That set me aback; she knew as well as I, she *had* to know, that it was not our plan to revive any heads, that nobody had the means to do so. 'Of course not,' I said.

'If you had, you'd have violated council wishes,' she said.

From the very beginning, she had me off balance. I tried to recover. 'We've broken no rules.'

'Council has been informed by a number of BMs' syndics that they're concerned about your activities.'

'You mean, they think we might try to bring more corpsicles up from Earth?'

'Yes,' she said, nodding once, firmly. 'That will not be allowed, if I have anything to do with it. Now, please explain what you plan to do with these heads.'

I was aghast. 'Excuse me? That's—'

'It's not confidential at all, Mickey. You've agreed to come here to speak with me. A great many BMs are awaiting my report on what you say.'

'That isn't what I understood, Fiona.' I tried to keep my voice calm. 'I'm not here testifying under oath, and I don't have to reveal family business plans to any council member, even the president.' I settled more firmly into my seat, trying to exude the confidence I had already scattered to the winds.

69

Her face hardened. 'It would be simple courtesy to your fellow BMs to explain what you intend to do, Mickey.'

I hoped to give her a tidbit sufficient to put her off. 'The heads are being preserved in the Ice Pit, in the void where my brother does his work.'

'Your brother-in-law, you mean.'

'Yes. He's family now. We dispense with such modifiers.' *When talking with outsiders*, I might have added.

She smiled, but her expression was still hard. 'William Pierce. He's doing BM-funded research on extremely low temperatures in copper, no?'

I nodded.

'Has he been successful?'

'Not yet,' I said.

'It's simple coincidence that his facilities are capable of preserving the heads?'

'I suppose so, yes. However, my sister probably would not have brought them to the Moon otherwise. But I think of it more as opportunity than coincidence.'

Fiona instructed the screens to bring up displays of lunar binding multiples who were pushing for an investigation of the Sandoval corpsicle imports. They were platinum names indeed: the top four BMs, except for Sandoval, and fifteen others, spaced around the Moon, including Nernst and Cailetet. 'Incidentally,' she said, 'You know about the furore on Earth.'

'I've heard,' I said.

'Did you know there's a ruckus starting on Mars now?'

I did not.

'They want Earth's dead kept on Earth,' the president said. 'They think it's bad precedent to export corpsicles and make the outer planets responsible for the inner's problems. They think the Moon must be siding with Earth in some fashion to get rid of this problem.'

'It's not a problem,' I said, exasperated. 'Nobody on Earth has made a fuss about this in decades.'

'So what's causing the fuss now?' she asked.

I tried to think my way through to a civil answer. 'We think Task-Felder is behind it,' I said.

'You accuse me of carrying my BM's interests into the council with me, despite my oath of office?'

'I'm not accusing anybody of anything,' I said. 'We have evidence that the representative, the ... the ... United States national assembly representative from Puerto Rico—'

'Congressional representative,' she corrected.

'Yes ... You know about that?'

'He's a Logologist. So is most of Puerto Rico. Are you accusing members of my religion of instigating this?'

She spoke with such complete shock and indignation that I thought for a moment, Could we be wrong? Were our facts misleading, poorly analysed? Then I remembered Janis Granger and her tactics in our first interview. Fiona Task-Felder was no more gentle, no more polite. I was here at her invitation to be raked over the coals.

'Excuse me, Madam President,' I said. 'I'd like for you to get to your point.'

'The point is, Mickey, that you've agreed by coming here to testify before the full council and explain your actions, your intentions, everything about this mess, at the next meeting, which will be in three days.'

I smiled and shook my head, then brought up my slate. 'Auto counsellor,' I said.

Her smile grew harder, her blue eyes more intense.

'Is this some new law you've cooked up for the occasion?' I asked, trying for a tough and sophisticated manner.

'Not at all,' she said with an air of closing claws on the kill. 'You may think what you wish about Task-Felder BM, or about Logologists – about my people – but we do not play outside the rules. Ask your auto counsellor about courtesy briefings and formal council meetings. This is a courtesy briefing, Mickey, and I've logged it as such.'

My auto counsellor found the relevant council rules on courtesy briefings, and the particular rule passed thirty years before, by the council, that mandated the council's right to hear just what the president heard, as testimony, under oath. A strange and parochial law, so seldom invoked that I had never heard of it. Until now.

71

'I'm ending this discussion,' I said, standing.

'Tell Thomas Sandoval-Rice that you and he should be at the next full council meeting. Under council agreements, you don't have any choice, Mickey.'

She did not smile. I left the office, walked quickly down the hall, avoided looking at anyone, especially the young women still moving files.

'She's snared her rabbit,' Thomas said as he poured me a beer.

He had been unusually quiet all evening, since I had announced myself at his door and made my anguished confession of gross ineptitude. Far worse than being blasted by his rage was facing his quiet disappointment. 'Don't blame yourself entirely, Micko.' He seemed somehow deflated, withdrawn, like an aquarium anemone touched by an uncaring finger. 'I should have guessed they'd try something like this.'

'I feel like an idiot.'

'That's the third time you've said that in the past ten minutes,' Thomas said. 'You have been an idiot, of course, but don't let that get you down.'

I shook my head; I was already down about as far as it was possible to fall.

Thomas lifted his beer, inspected the large bubbles, and said, 'If we don't testify, we're in much worse trouble. It will look as if we're ignoring the wishes of our fellow BMs, as if we've gone renegade. If we do testify, we'll have been manoeuvred into breaking the BMs' sacred right to keep business and research matters private . . . and that will make us look like weaklings and fools. She's pushed us into a deep rille, Mickey. If you had refused to go in, and had claimed family privilege, she'd have tried something else . . .

'At least now we can be sure what we're in store for. Isolation, recrimination, probable withdrawal of contracts, maybe even boycott of services. That's never happened before, Micko. We're going to make history this week, no doubt about it.'

'Is there anything I can do?'

Thomas finished his glass and wiped his lips. 'Another?' he asked, gesturing at the keg. I shook my head. 'No. Me neither. We need clear heads, Micko, and we need a full family meeting. We're going to have to build internal solidarity here; this has gone way beyond what the director and all the syndics can handle by themselves.'

I flew back from Port Yin, head cloudy with anguish. It seemed somehow I had been responsible for all of this. Thomas did not say as much, not this time; but he had hinted it before. I halfway hoped the shuttle would smear itself across the regolith; that the pilot would survive and I would not. Then, anguish began to be replaced by a grim and determined anger. I had been twisted around by experts; used by those who had no qualms about use and abuse. I had seen the enemy and underestimated the strength of their resolve, whatever their motivations, whatever their goals. These people were not following the lunar way; they were playing us all – all of the BMs, me, Rho, the Triple, the Western Hemispheric United States, the corpsicles – like fish on a line, single-mindedly dedicated to one end.

The heads were just an excuse. They had no real importance; that much was obvious.

This was a power play. The Logologists were intent on dominating the Moon, perhaps the Earth. I hated them for their ambition, their evil presumption, for the way they had lowered me in the eyes of Thomas.

Having erred on the side of underestimation, I was now swinging in the opposite direction, equally in error; but I would not realize that for a few more days yet.

I came home, and knew for the first time how much the station meant to me.

I met a Cailetet man in the alley leading to the Ice Pit. 'You're Mickey, right?' he asked casually. He held a small silver case in front of him, dangling from one hand. He seemed happy. I looked at him as if he might utter words of absolute betrayal.

'We've just investigated one of your heads,' he said, only slightly put off by my expression. 'You've been shuttling, eh?'

I nodded. 'How's Rho?' I asked, somewhat irrelevantly; I hadn't spoken to anybody since my arrival.

'She's ecstatic, I think. We've done our work well.'

'You're sticking with us?' I asked suspiciously.

'Beg your pardon?'

'You haven't been recalled by your family syndics?'

'No,' he said, drawling the word dubiously. 'Not that I've heard.'

The families were being incredibly two-faced. 'Just curious,' I said. 'What's it going to cost us?'

'In the long term? That's *right*,' he said, as if the reason for my surliness had finally been solved. 'You're financial manager for the Ice Pit. I'm sorry; I'm a bit slow. Believe me, we're interested in this as a research project. If we perfect our techniques here, we can market the medical applications all over the Triple and beyond. We're charging you expenses and nothing else, Mickey. This is platinum opportunity.'

'Does it work?' I asked, still sullen.

He thumped the case. 'Data right here. We're checking it with history on Earth. I'd say it works, yes. Talking with the dead – I don't think anybody's done that before!'

'Who was it?' I asked.

'One of the three unknowns. Rho decided we'd work with them first, to help solve the mystery. Please go right in, Mickey. Nernst has designed a very nice facility. Ask questions, see what they're doing. They're working on unknown number two right now.'

'Thanks,' I said, wondering what distortion of protocol could lead this man to invite me into my own BM's facility. 'I'm glad it's working.'

'All right,' the man said, with a short intake of breath. 'Must be off. Check this individual out, correlate . . . on our own nickel, Mickey. Good to have met you.'

I stopped at the white line and queried. 'Goddamn it, yes!' William's voice roared from the speaker. 'It's open. Just cross the goddamn line and stop bothering me.'

'It's me, Mickey,' I said.

'Well then, come on in and join the party! Everybody else is here.'

William had locked himself in the laboratory. Three Onnes and Cailetet techs were on the bridge, standing well away from the force disorder pumps, chatting and eating lunch. I passed them by with casual nods.

William sounded in no mood for visitors – this time of day was usually his phase of most intense activity. I swung on to the lift and descended to Rho's facility, twenty feet below the laboratory. The Ice Pit echoed with voices from above and below; the sounds seemed to come from all directions as I descended in the open lift, first to the right, then the left, cancelled, returned, grew soft, then immediate. Rho came through the hatch at the top of the chamber and rushed forward excitedly. 'William's pissed off, but we're leaving him alone, mostly, so it will pass.' She fairly brewed over with enthusiasm. '*Oh, Mickey!*' She threw her arms around me.

'Yes?'

'Did you hear upstairs? We tuned in to a head! It works! Come on in. We're working on the second head now.'

'An unknown,' I said with polite interest, her enthusiasm not infecting me. (How much could I blame *her* for these problems?)

'Yes. Another unknown. I still can't get a response from the StarTime trustees. Do you think they've lost all their back-up records? That would be something, wouldn't it?' She ushered me down the hatch into the chamber. Within the chamber, all was quiet but for a faint song of electronics and the low hiss of refrigerants.

I recognized Armand Cailetet-Davis, the balding, slight-figured powerhouse of Cailetet research. Beside him stood Irma Stolbart of Onnes, a reputed lunar-born superwhiz whom I had heard of but never met: thirty or thirty-five,

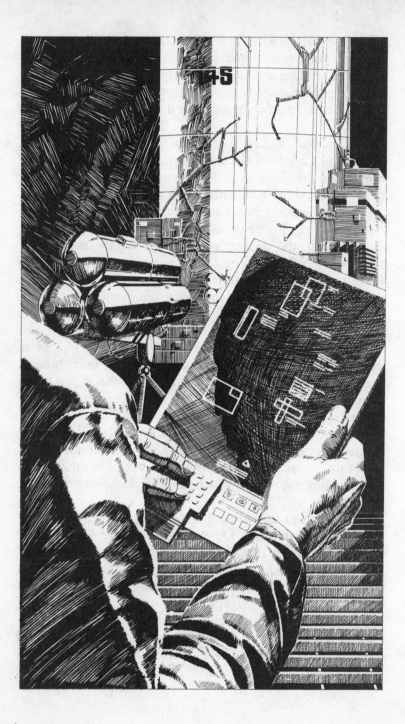

tall and thin with reddish brown hair and chocolate skin. They stood beside a tripod-mounted piece of equipment, three horizontal cylinders strapped together, pointed at the face of one of the forty stainless-steel boxes mounted in the racks.

Rho introduced me to Cailetet-Davis and Stolbart. I felt a little thrill of something – a realization of what was actually going on here – penetrating my dark mood.

'We're selecting one of the seventy-three known natural mind languages,' Armand explained, pointing at a thinker prism in Irma Stolbart's hands. She smiled, quick glance at me, at Armand, distracted, then continued to work on her thinker, which was about a tenth the size of William's QL, easily portable. 'We'll test some uploaded data for patterns—'

'Patterns from the head,' I said, stating the obvious.

'Yes. A masculine individual, age sixty-five at death, apparently in good condition considering the medical standards of the time. Very little deterioration.'

'Have you looked inside?' I asked.

Rho lifted her brows. 'Brother, nobody looks inside. Not by actually opening the box. We don't care what they *look* like.' She laughed nervously. 'It's not the head, it's what's locked up in the brain.'

A *soul, still?* Now I was shivering from fatigue, as well as something like superstitious awe. 'Sorry,' I said to nobody in particular. They ignored me, concentrating on their work.

'We find northern Europeans tend to cluster in these three program areas,' Stolbart explained. She showed me a slate screen on which a diagram had been sketched. The diagram showed twelve different rectangles, each labelled with a cultural-ethnic group. Her finger underlined three boxes: *Finn/ Scand/ Teut/.* 'Mind memory-storage languages are among the genetic traits most rigidly adhered to. We think they change very little across thousands of years. That makes sense, considering the necessity of immediate infant adaptation to its milieu.'

'Indeed,' Rho said, smiling at me, squeezing my arm again gently. 'So he's of northern European stock?'

'He's definitely not Levantine, African or Oriental,' Irma Stolbart said. I watched her curiously, focusing on her face, lean and intent, with lovely, sceptical brown eyes.

'Have you spoken with your syndics?' I asked out of the blue, startling even myself.

Armand had clearly earned his position in Cailetet through quick thinking and adaptability. With no hesitation whatsoever, he said, 'We work here until somebody tells us to leave. Nobody has yet. Maybe you administrators can work it all out in the council.'

You administrators. That put us in our place. Paper pushers, bureaucrats, politicians. Cut the politics. We were the ones who stood in the way of the scientist's goal of unrestrained research and intellection.

'I see a fourteen Penrose cipher trace algorithm in the cerebral cortex,' Irma said. 'Definitely northern European.'

Rho looked troubled, examined my face for signs. With a tug of my ear and a gesture up into the air I indicated we should talk. She drew me aside. 'Are you tired?' she asked.

'Dead on my feet,' I said. 'I'm an idiot, Rho, and maybe I've augered this whole thing right into a rille.'

'I have faith in the family. We'll make it. I have faith in you, Micko,' she said, grasping my arm. I felt vaguely sick, seeing her expression of support, her trust. 'I'd like you to stay and watch . . . this is really something . . . if you're up to it?'

'Wouldn't miss it,' I said.

'It's almost religious, isn't it?' she whispered in my ear.

'All right,' Armand said. 'We have the locale. Let's take a picture, upload into the translator, and see if we can draw a name from the file.'

Armand adjusted the position on the triple cylinders and tuned his slate to their output, getting a picture of a vague grey mass suspended by a thin sling in a sharp black square – the head resting in its cubicle and cradle within the larger box. 'We're centred,' he said. 'Irma, if you could . . .'

'Field guide on,' she said, flipping a switch on a tiny disk taped to the box.

'Recording,' Armand said nonchalantly. There was no noise, no visible or audible sign that anything was happening. Squares appeared on Armand's slate in the upper right-hand portion of the mass. I was able to make out that the head had slumped to one side, whether facing us or not, I could not tell. I kept staring at the image, the squares flashing one by one in sequence around the cranium, and I realized with a gruesome tingle that the head was misshapen, that during its decades in storage it had deformed in the presence of Earth gravity, nestling deeper into its sling like a frozen melon.

'Got it,' Armand said. 'One more – the third unknown – and we'll call it a session.'

For Rho's sake, I stayed to watch the third head being scanned and its neural states and patterns recorded. I kissed Rho's cheek, congratulated her and took the lift to the bridge. Again, the voices flowed around me, soft technical chatter from the chamber below, the technicians on the bridge above.

I went to my water tank room and collapsed.

Strangely enough, I slept well.

Rho came into my room and woke me up at twelve hundred, eight hours after I'd dropped on to my bed. Obviously, she had not slept at all; her hair was matted with finger-tugs and rearrangement, her face shiny with long hours.

'We got a name on the number one unknown,' she said. 'It's a female, not a male, we think. But we haven't done chromosome check through their sensors. Irma located a few minutes of pre-death short-term memory and translated it into sound. We heard . . .' She suddenly wrinkled her face, as if about to cry, and then lifted her head and laughed. 'Micko, we *heard* a voice, it must have been a doctor, a voice speaking out loud, "Inchmore, can you hear me? Evelyn? We need your permission . . ." '

79

I sat up on the bed and rubbed my eyes. 'That's. . . .' I couldn't find a good word.

'Yeah, amen,' Rho said, sitting on the edge of the bed. 'Evelyn Inchmore. I've sent a query to StarTime's trustees on Earth. Evelyn Inchmore, Evelyn Inchmore. . . .' She spoke the name out loud several more times, her voice dropping in exhaustion and wonder. 'Do you know what this means, Micko?'

'Congratulations,' I said.

'It's the first time anybody has ever communicated with a corpsicle,' Rho said distantly.

'She hasn't answered back,' I said. 'You've just accessed her memories.' I shrugged my shoulders. 'She's still dead.'

'Yeah,' Rho said. '*Just* accessed her memories. Wait a minute.' She looked up at me, startled by some inner realization. 'Maybe it's a male, after all. We thought the name was female. . . . But didn't Evelyn used to be a male's name? Wasn't there a male author centuries ago named Evelyn?'

'Evelyn Waugh,' I said. 'Long E.'

'We could have it all wrong again,' she said, too tired to build up much concern. 'I hope we can straighten it out before this goes to the press.'

My level of alertness went up several notches. 'Have you told Thomas what's happened?'

'Not yet,' she said.

'Rho, if word gets out that we've already accessed the heads. . . . But who's going to stop Cailetet or Onnes from trumpeting this?'

'You think it would cause problems?' Rho asked.

I felt vaguely proud that finally I was starting to anticipate trouble, as Thomas would want me to. 'It would probably cook off the bomb,' I said.

'All right, then. I don't want to cause more trouble than is absolutely necessary.' She looked at me with loving sympathy. 'You've been in a rough, Micko.'

'You heard what happened in Port Yin?'

'Thomas talked to me while you were shuttling home.' She pushed out her lips dubiously and shook her head.

80

'Fapping pol. Someone should impeach her and take away the Task-Felder charter.'

'I appreciate the sentiments, but neither is likely. Could you keep this quiet for a few more days?'

'I'll do my damnedest,' Rho said. 'Cailetet and Onnes are under contract. We control the release of the results, even if they get full scientific credit. I'll tell them we want to confirm with the Earth trustees, back up our findings, analyse the third unknown head ... work on a few known heads and see if the process is reliable.'

'What about Great-Grandmother and Great-Grandfather?' I asked.

Rho's smile was conspiratorial. 'We'll save them until later,' she said.

'We don't want to experiment on family, right?'

She nodded. 'When we're sure the whole thing works, we'll do something with Robert and Emilia. As for me, Micko, in a few minutes I'm going to get some induced sleep. Right after I lay down some rules to the Cailetet and Onnes folks. Now, William wants to talk with you.'

'About the interruptions?'

'I don't think so. He says work is going well.'

She hugged me tightly and then stood. 'To sleep,' she said. 'No dreams, I think ...'

'No ancient voices,' I said.

'Right.'

William seemed tired but at peace, pleased with himself. He sat in the laboratory control centre, patting the QL thinker as if it were an old friend.

'It did me proud, Micko,' he said. 'It's tuned everything to a fare-thee-well. It keeps the universe's quantum bugs from nibbling at my settings, controls the rebuilt disorder pumps, anticipates virtual fluctuations and corrects for them. I'm all set now; all I have to do is bring the pumps to full capacity.'

I tried to show enthusiasm, but couldn't. I felt sick at heart. The disaster in Port Yin, the upcoming council meeting, Rho's success with the first few heads ...

With a little time to think about what had happened, I realized now that it all felt *bad*. Thomas was scrambling furiously to convince the council to reverse its action. And here I was, cut out of the drift of things, watching William gloat about an upcoming moment of triumph. William caught my mood and reached out to tap my hand.

'Hey,' he said. 'You're young. Fapping up is part of the game.'

I screwed my face up at first in anger, then in simple grief, and turned away, tears running down my cheeks. To have William name the card so openly – *fapping up* – was not what I needed right now. It was neither circumspect nor sensitive. 'Thank you so very much,' I said.

William kept tapping my hand until I jerked it away. 'I'm sorry, Micko,' he said, his tone unchanged – telling it like it is. 'I've never been afraid to admit when I've made a mistake. It nearly drives me nuts sometimes, making mistakes. I keep telling myself I should be perfect, but that isn't what we're here for. Perfection isn't an option for us; perfection is death, Micko. We're here to learn and change, and that means making mistakes.'

'Thanks for the lecture,' I said, glancing at him resentfully.

'I'm twelve years older than you are. I've made maybe twelve times more major mistakes. What can I tell you? That it gets any easier to fap up? Well, yes, it gets easier and easier with more and more responsibilities – but hell, Micko, it doesn't feel any better.'

'I can't just think of it as a mistake,' I said softly. 'I was betrayed. The president was dishonest and underhanded.'

William leaned back in his chair and shook his head, incredulous. 'Hay-soos, Micko. Who expects anything different? That's what politics is all about – coercion and lies.'

Suddenly my anger reached white heat. 'Goddamn it, *no*, that isn't what politics is all about, William, and people thinking that it is has gotten us into this mess!'

'I don't understand.'

'Politics is management and guidance and feedback, William. We seem to have forgotten *that* on the Moon.

82

Politics is the art of managing large groups of people in good times and bad. When the people know what they want and when they don't know what they want. "Cut the politics. . . ." Hay-soos yourself, William!' I waved my arm out and shook my fist in the air. 'You can't get rid of politics, any more than you can. . . .' I struggled to find a metaphor. 'Any more than you can cut out *manners* and *talking* and all the other ways we interact.'

'Thanks for the lecture, Micko,' William said, not unpleasantly.

I dropped my fist on the table.

'What you're saying is, the whole Moon is screwing this up,' William said. 'I agree. And the Task-Felder BM is leading us all into temptation. But my point is, I'm never going to be a politician or an administrator. Present company excepted, I hate the breed, Micko. They're put on this Moon to stand in my way. This council stuff only reinforces my prejudices. So what can you do about it?' He looked at me with frank inquiry.

'I can wise up,' I said. 'I can be a better . . . administrator, politician.'

William smiled ironically. 'More devious? Play their own game?'

I shook my head. Deviousness and playing the Task-Felder game were not what I meant. I was thinking of some more idealistic superiority, playing within the ethical boundaries as well as the law.

William continued. 'We can plan ahead for the worst yet to come. They might cut off our resources, beyond just stopping other BMs from helping us. We can survive an interdict for some time, maybe even forge a separate business alliance within the Triple.'

'That would be . . . very dangerous,' I said.

'If we're forced into it, what can we do? We have business interests all over the Triple. We have to survive.'

The QL toned softly on the platform. 'Temperature stability has been broken,' it said.

William jerked up in his chair. 'Report,' he said.

83

'Unknown effect has caused temperature to rotate in unknown phase. The cells have no known temperature at this time.'

'What's that mean?' I asked.

William grabbed his thinker remote and pushed through the curtain to the bridge. He walked out to the Cavity and I followed, glad to have an interruption. The Cailetet and Onnes techs had retired to get some rest; the Ice Pit was quiet.

'What's wrong?' I asked.

'I don't know,' William said in a low voice, concentrating on the Cavity's status display. 'There are drains on four of the eight cells. The QL refuses to interpret temperature readings. QL, please explain.'

The remote said, 'Phase rotation in lambda. Fluctuation between banks of four cells.'

'Shit,' William said. 'Now the other four cells are absorbing, and the first four are stable. QL, do you have any idea what's happening here?' He looked up at me with a worried expression.

'Second bank is now in down cycle of rotation. Up cycle in three seconds.'

'It's reversed,' William said after the short interval had passed. 'Back and forth. QL, what's causing a power drain?'

'Temperature maintenance,' the QL said.

'Explain, please,' William pursued with waning patience.

'Energy is being accepted by the phase down cells in an attempt to maintain temperature.'

'Not by the refrigerators or the pumps?'

'It is necessary to put energy directly into the cells in the form of microwave radiation to try to maintain temperature.'

'I don't understand, QL.'

'I apologize,' the QL said. 'The cells accept radiation to remain stable, but they have no temperature this thinker can interpret.'

'We have to *raise* the temperature?' William guessed, face slack with incredulity.

'Phase down reversal,' the QL said.

84

'QL, the temperatures have jumped to *below* absolute zero?'

'That is an interpretation, although not a very good one.'

William swore and stood back from the Cavity.

The QL reported, 'All eight cells have stabilized in lambda phase down. Fluctuation has stopped.'

William went pale. 'Micko, tell me I'm not dreaming.'

'I don't know what the hell you're doing,' I said, starting to become frightened.

'The cells are draining microwave energy and maintaining a stable temperature. Christ, they must be accessing new spin dimensions, radiating into a direction outside status geometry. . . . Does that mean they're operating in negative time? Micko, if any of Rho's outsiders have messed with the lab, or if their goddamn equipment is causing this. . . .' He balled his fists up and shook them at the darkness above. 'God help them! I was this close, Micko. . . . All I had to do was connect the pumps, align the cells, turn the magnetic fields off. . . . I was going to do that tomorrow.'

'I don't think anybody's messed with your equipment,' I told him, trying to calm him. 'These are pros, William, and besides, Rho would kill them.'

William lowered his head and swung it back and forth helplessly. 'Micko, something has to be wrong. Negative temperature is meaningless.'

'It didn't *say* temperatures were negative,' I reminded him.

'This thinker does not interpret the data,' the QL chimed in.

'That's because you're a coward,' William accused it.

'This thinker does not relay false interpretation,' it responded.

Suddenly, William laughed, a rocking, angry laugh that seemed to hurt. He opened his eyes wide and patted the QL remote with gritted-teeth paternalism. 'Micko, as God is my witness, nothing on this Moon is ever easy, no?'

'Maybe you've got something even more important than absolute zero,' I suggested. 'A new state of matter.'

85

The idea sobered him. 'That. . . .' He ran his hand through his hair, making it even more unruly. 'A big idea, that.'

'Need help?' I asked.

'I need time to think,' he said softly. 'Thanks, Micko. I need time without interruptions . . . a few hours at least.'

'I can't guarantee anything,' I said.

He squinted at me. 'I'll let you know if I've discovered something big, okay? Now get out of here.' He pushed me gently along the bridge.

The Council Room was circular, panelled with lunar farm oak, centrally lighted, with a big antique display screen at one end, lovingly preserved from the year of the council's creation. Politicians like to keep an eye on each other; no corners, no chairs facing away from the centre.

I shuffled in behind Thomas and two freelance advocates from Port Yin, hired by Thomas to offer him extrafamilial advice. Within the Triple it has often been said that lunar advocates are the very worst money can rent; there is some truth to that, but Thomas still felt the need of an objective and critical point of view.

The room was mostly empty. Three representatives had already taken their seats – interestingly enough, they were from Cailetet, Onnes and Nernst BMs. Other representatives talked in the hall outside the room. The president and her staff would not enter until just before the meeting began.

The council thinker, a large, antique terrestrial model encased in grey ceramic, rested below the president's dais at the north end of the room. Thomas nudged me as we sat, pointed at the thinker and said, 'Don't underestimate an old machine. That son of a glitch has more experience in this room than anybody. But it's the president's tool, not ours; it will not contradict the president, and it will not speak out against her.'

We sat quietly while the room slowly filled. At the appointed time of commencement, Fiona Task-Felder entered through a door behind the president's dais, Janis

86

Granger and three council advocates in train.

I knew many of the BM representatives. I had spoken to ten or fifteen of them over the years while doing research for my minor; others I knew by sight from lunar news reports and council broadcasts. They were honourable women and men all; I thought we might not do so badly here after all.

Thomas's expression revealed a less favourable opinion.

The Ice Pit controversy was not first on the council agenda. There were matters of who would get contracts to parent lucrative volatiles supply deliveries from the outer planets; who had rights in a BM border dispute to sell aluminium and tungsten mining claims to Richter BM, the huge and generally silent tri-family merger that had taken over most lunar mining operations. These problems were discussed by the representatives in a way that struck me as exemplary. Resolutions were reached, contracts vetted and cleared, shares assigned. The president remained silent most of the time. When she did speak, her words were well-chosen and to the point. She impressed me.

Thomas seemed to sink into his chair, chin in hand, grey hair in disarray. He glanced at me once, gave me something like a leer, and retreated into glum contemplation.

Our two outside advocates sat plumbline in their chairs, hardly blinking.

Janis Granger read out the next item on the agenda: 'Inter-family disputes regarding purchase by Sandoval BM of human remains from terrestrial preservation societies.'

Socie*ties*. That was a subtlety that could speak volumes of misinterpretation. Thomas closed his eyes, opened them again after a long moment.

'The representative from Gorrie BM would like to address this issue,' the president said. 'Chair allots five minutes to Achmed Bani Sadr of Gorrie BM.'

Thomas straightened, leaned forward. Bani Sadr stood with slate held at waist-level for prompting.

'The syndics of Gorrie BM have expressed some concern over the strain on Triple relations this purchase might provoke. As the major transportation utility between Earth and Moon, and on many translunar links, our business would be very adversely affected by any shift in terrestrial attitudes . . .'

And so it began. Even I in my naivety could see that this had been brilliantly orchestrated. One by one, politely, the BMs stood in council and voiced their collective concern. Earth had rattled its pocketbooks at us; Mars had chided us for rocking the Triple boat in a time of economic instability. The United States of the Western Hemisphere had voted to restrict lunar trade if this matter was not resolved to its satisfaction.

Thomas's expression was intense, sorrowful but alert. He had not been inactive. Cailetet had expressed an interest in pursuing potentially very lucrative, even revolutionary, research on the deceased; Onnes BM testified that there was no conceivable way these heads could be resurrected and made active members of society within the next twenty years; the technology simply did not yet exist, despite decades of promising research.

Surprisingly, the representative from Gorrie BM reversed himself and expressed an interest in the medical aspects of this research; he asked how long such work might take to mature, in a business sense, but the president – not unreasonably – ruled that this was beyond the scope of the present discussion.

The representative from Richter BM expressed sympathy for Sandoval's attempts to open a new field of lunar business, but said that disturbances in lunar raw materials supply lines to Earth could be disastrous in the short term. 'If Earth boycotts lunar minerals, the outer planets can supply them almost immediately, and we lose one-third of our gross lunar export business.'

Thomas requested time to speak in reply. The president granted him ten minutes to state Sandoval's case.

He conferred briefly with the advocates. They nodded agreement to several whispered comments, and he stood, slate at waist-level, the formal posture in this room, to begin his reply.

'Madam President, honoured Representatives, I'll be brief, and I'll be blunt. I am ashamed of these proceedings, and I am ashamed that this council has been so blind as to make them necessary. I have never, in my thirty-nine years of service to the Sandoval BM, and in my seventy-five years of lunar citizenship, felt the anguish I feel now, knowing what is about to happen. Knowing what is about to be done to lunar ideals in the name of expediency.

'Sandoval BM has made an entirely reasonable business transaction with a fully authorized terrestrial legal entity. For reasons none of us can fathom, Task-Felder BM, and Madam President, have raised a flare of protest and carefully planned and executed a series of manoeuvres to force an autonomous lunar family to divest itself of legally acquired resources. To my knowledge, this has never before been attempted in the history of the Moon.'

'You speak of actions not yet taken, perhaps not even contemplated,' the president said.

Thomas looked around the room and smiled. 'Madam President, I address those who have already received their instructions.'

'Are you accusing the president of participating in this so-called conspiracy?' Fiona Task-Felder continued.

Calls of 'Let him speak', 'Let him have his say'. She nodded and motioned for Thomas to resume.

'I have not much more to say, but to recount a tale of masterful politics, conducted by an extralunar organization across the solar system, in support of a policy that has nothing to do with lunar well-being or business. Even my assistant, Mickey Sandoval, has been trapped into giving testimony on private family affairs, through a ruse involving an old council law not invoked since its creation. My fellow citizens, he will testify under protest if this council so wishes – but think of the precedent! Think of the power you give to this council, and to those who have the skills to manipulate it – skills which we have not ourselves acquired, and are not likely to acquire, because such activity goes against our basic nature. We are naive weaklings in such a fight, and because of our

89

weakness, our lack of foresight and planning, we will give in, and my family's activities will be interfered with, perhaps even forbidden – all because a religious organization, based on our home planet, does not wish us to do things we have every legal right to do. I voice my protest now, that it may be put in the record before the council votes. Our shame will be complete by day's end, Madam President, and I will not wish to show my face in these chambers thereafter.'

The president's face was cold and pale. 'Do you accuse me, or my chartered BM, of being controlled by extralunar interests?'

Thomas, who had sat quickly after his short talk, stood again, looked around the council and nodded curtly. 'I do.'

'It is not traditional to libel one's fellow BMs in this council,' the president said.

Thomas did not answer.

'I believe I must reply to the charge of manipulation. At my invitation, Mickey Sandoval came to Port Yin to render voluntary testimony to the president. Under old council rules, designed to prevent the president from keeping information that rightfully should be given to the council, the president has the duty to request testimony be given to the council as a whole. If that is manipulation, then I am guilty.'

Our first extrafamilial advocate stood up beside Thomas. 'Madam President, a tape of Mickey Sandoval's visit to your office is sufficient to fulfil the requirements of that rule.'

'Not according to the council thinker's interpretation,' the president said. 'Please render your judgment.'

The thinker spoke. 'The spirit of the rule is to encourage more open testimony to the council than to the president in private meetings. A voluntary report to the president implies willingness to testify in full to the council. Such testimony must always be voluntary, and not under threat of subpoena.' Its deep, resonating voice left the council room in silence.

'So much for our auto counsellors,' the first advocate muttered to Thomas. Again he addressed the council. 'Mickey Sandoval's testimony was solicited under guise of casual conversation. He was not aware he would later be forced to divulge family business matters to the entire council.'

'The president's conversations on council matters can hardly be called casual. I am not concerned with your assistant's lack of education,' the president said. 'This council deserves to hear Sandoval BM's plans for these deceased individuals.'

'In God's name, why?' Thomas stood, jaw outthrust. 'Who asks these questions? Why is private Sandoval business of concern to anybody but us?'

The president did not react as strongly to this outburst as I expected. I cringed, but Fiona Task-Felder said, 'The freedom of any family to swing its fist ends at our nose. How the inquiry has arisen is irrelevant; what *is* relevant is the damage that might occur to lunar interests. Is that enough, Mr Sandoval-Rice?'

Thomas sat down without answering. I looked at him curiously; how much of this was show, how much loss of control? Seeing his expression, I realized that show and inner turmoil were one. Only then did I understand, gut-level, that he knew things I did not know, and that our situation was truly desperate. Thomas was a consummate and seasoned professional syndic, a true lunar citizen in the old sense of concerned and responsible free spirit, quickly losing his few illusions as to power and government and lunar politics.

I turned my gaze to the president's dais, to Fiona Task-Felder, feeling for the first time a flash of real hatred. I date my present self to that moment; it was as if I had been reborn, more cynical, more calculating, sharper, no longer young. My hands trembled. I made them still, wiped their dampness on my pants, swiftly calculated what I might give in testimony and what I might withhold.

The representative from Richter BM stood and was recognized by Janis Granger. 'Madam President, I move that we have Mr Mickey Sandoval stand forward and testify, as required by the rules, but that Mr Sandoval's testimony be restricted to those areas that will not reveal information that could adversely affect future profit potential for his family. That is, should this council vote to allow the project to continue.'

Thomas's expression brightened the merest of a mere. I hoped for the president to falter, to acknowledge this limitation to her success, but she hardly blinked an eye before saying, 'Is there a second?'

Cailetet and Nernst reps seconded in unison. A quick vote was taken and the decision was unanimous; even the Task-Felder rep joined the flow.

This was the first block in the path of the juggernaut. It was a small block; it was quickly crushed; but it provided us with an immense amount of needed relief.

I testified, following an outline quickly prepared by Thomas and vetted by the advocates; the council listened attentively. I did not discuss our success in deciphering some of the mental contents of one of the dead.

The Task-Felder rep stood at the end of my testimony and urged the council to vote now on whether our project would continue. The motion was seconded. Thomas did not object or ask for delay.

Cailetet, Nernst and Onnes voted for the project to continue.

The remaining fifty-one reps voted for the project to be shut down.

History was made, political paradigms shifted, all according to the rules.

After adjournment, Thomas and I went out to a Port Yin pub and sat over two schooners of fresh ale, saying very little for the first five minutes.

'Not so bad,' Thomas commented after draining the last of his glass. 'We didn't go down in glorious flames. Bless massive old Richter; draw and quarter us, but leave us our dignity before we're spiked.'

'I don't want to tell Rho,' I said.

'She already knows, Mickey. My office has called the Ice Pit. She wants to talk with you, but I don't want you to talk to anyone until we chat a while. All right?'

I nodded.

'Do I detect a change in your attitudes?' Thomas asked gently.

I smiled. 'Yes. And in yours?'

'I'm not as good a syndic as you might believe, Micko.' He waved off my weak objection. 'Save it for your memoirs. I couldn't stop this. But I can delay the results. The council is going to have to design a plan for us, some way to end the project with minimal loss of resources. That will take a few weeks, and I don't think Task-Felder – Fiona or her BM – can speed things up. I'll make sure they don't, if I have to resort to assassination.'

He didn't smile. In my present frame of mind, I didn't care whether he was serious or not.

'You know, Micko, I've always had my doubts about this project. I think the reasons we lost in the council are less political and more psychological, perhaps even mystical. Deep down, I think they believe – and maybe even I believe – we're interfering where we shouldn't. If Rho succeeds, it's going to change a lot of things. We're a peculiar kind of conservative lot here on the Moon, spiritually, however much we keep our religious observances to ourselves.'

'She has,' I said.

'She has what?'

'Succeeded. They have, actually.'

'Yes?'

'They've accessed a head. They're working on a second head now. We know their names. We—'

My face contorted and I shivered, cursed, half-stood. Something walked over my future grave; I almost literally saw a ghost sitting beside us at the table, the image of an immensely fat Pharaoh covered with ice, watching us all balefully. Thomas reached out to take hold of my arm and I sat. The ghost was gone.

'Don't lose it now, Mickey,' Thomas said. Other customers stared at us. 'What's wrong?'

'Christ, I don't know. Thomas, I've got to go back. To the Ice Pit. Something just occurred to me, something really bad.'

'Can you tell me?'

'Hell, no,' I said, shaking my head. 'It's too stupid and wild. But I have to go back.' I stood. 'Please forgive me. It's a hunch, a ridiculous hunch.'

'You're forgiven,' Thomas said, and credited the tab to his personal account.

I caught the regular Ice Pit shuttle; luck and the timetable were on my side. I was in a fever of inspired unease. I could not shake my theory. My head spun with disbelief; this could not be, yet it all fitted together so smoothly, yet again the chances were more than astronomical; and I realized that if I were wrong, and I had to be, no doubt about it, I wouldn't be worthy of my position in the Sandoval BM. I would have to resign. If I played such wild hunches, if I could become so obsessed by them, I was a useless crank.

We flew over the external generation plant, a bright red building against pale grey dust and rock. The shuttle banked over the Ice Pit radiators, hunkering in their shadowy trenches, glowing dull red-orange as they broadcast heat into the darkness of space.

We landed and I disembarked, small case in hand. I was eight hours past reasonable sleep time but did not stop to stimulate or simulate. I barely took time to drop my case off in my water tank.

I rang up Rho, waking her.

'Have they pulled their equipment yet?' I asked.

'Who?' she responded sleepily. 'Stolbart and Cailetet-Davis? No. They're waiting to get orders from their BMs. Thomas said you'd fill me in on some things – he was going to talk with you.'

'Yes, well there are delays, and I have to do some research. Have you accessed the third head yet?'

'We've downloaded some patterns, but they're not translated. This mess has kind of put a crimp in our enthusiasm, Micko.'

'I understand. Rho, get them to translate what you have.'

'You sound a bit crazed, brother. Don't take this personally. This is my screw-up, not yours. Tulips, remember?'

'Just get those patterns translated. Please. Humour me.'

I leaned back in my chair, stunned by all that was happening, assessing my position, our position, if my hunch was correct.

Then I began yet more research. There was no way around it – what I needed to know would very likely be found only on Earth, and it would cost me dearly.

I would charge it to my personal account.

I crossed the white line six hours later. I still hadn't slept. My world of warrens and alleys and water tanks and volcanic bubbles and bridges and force disorder pumps was taking on a quality of bitter dream; I do not know why I felt William was the still point in the centre of my life, but he was, and I needed above all else to find out how his project was proceeding. There seemed something almost holy and pure in his quest, above human conflict; I sensed I could take comfort in his presence, in his words.

But William himself was not comfortable. He looked a wreck. He, too, had not slept. I entered the laboratory, ignoring the soft voices from the chamber below, and found him standing by the QL thinker, eyes closed, lips moving as if in prayer. He opened his eyes and faced me with a jerk of his shoulders and head. 'Christ,' he said softly. 'Are they done down there?'

I shook my head. 'I'm afraid I've set them on to something new.'

'I heard you've been checkmated,' he said.

I shrugged. 'And you?'

'My opponent is far more subtle than any human conspiracy,' he said. 'I've gone so far as to be able to switch between plus and minus.' He chuckled. 'I can access this new state at will, but there's real resistance to reaching the no-man's-land between. I have the QL cogitating now. It's been working five hours on the problem.'

'What's the problem?' I asked.

'Micko, I haven't even engaged the force disorder pumps to achieve this new state. No magnetic field cut-off, no special efforts – just a sudden jerk-down to this negative state, absorbing energy to maintain an undefined temperature.'

'But why?'

'The best the QL can come up with is we're approaching some key event that sends signals back in time, affecting our experiment now.'

'So neither of you know what's actually happened?'

He shook his head. 'It's not only undefined, it's incomprehensible. Even the QL is befuddled by it and can't give me straight answers.'

I sat on the edge of the QL's platform and caressed the machine with an open palm as if in sympathy. 'Everything's screwed, top to bottom,' I said. 'The centre cannot hold.'

'Ah, Micko – there's the question. What is the centre? What is this event we're approaching that can reach subtle fingers back and befuddle us now?'

I smiled. 'We're a real pair of loons,' I said.

'Speak for yourself,' William said defensively, prickly. 'I'll solve this dustover, by God, Micko.' He pointed down. 'Solve your little problem, and I'll solve mine.'

As if on cue, Rho stood in the open laboratory door, face ashen. 'Mickey,' she said. 'How did you know?'

The shock of confirmation – and confirmation was not in doubt – made me tremble. I glanced at William. 'A little ghost told me. A fat nightmare on ice.'

'We don't have too much translated,' she said. 'But we know his name.'

'What are you talking about?' William asked.

'Our third unknown,' I explained. 'We have three unknown heads below, three among four hundred and ten. Alleged bad record-keeping.'

'Do you know something, Mickey?' Rho asked.

'There were four Logologists employed by StarTime Preservation between 2079 and 2094,' I said. 'Two worked in records, two were in administration. None were ever given access to the heads themselves; they were kept in cold vaults in Denver.'

'You think they screwed up the records?'

'It was the most they could manage.'

'It's so *cynical*,' Rho said. 'I can't believe such a thing. It would be like our . . . trying to kill Robert and Emilia. It's sickening.'

William uttered a wordless curse of frustration. 'Dammit, Rho, what are you talking about?'

'We know why we're having such problems with Task-Felder. I've hit the jackpot, William. I've brought a real wolf into our fold. I apologize.'

'What wolf?'

'K. D. Thierry,' I said, the breath going out of me. I didn't know whether I might laugh or cry.

'You've got *him* down there?' William asked.

Rho and I hugged each other and laughed, near hysteria. 'Kimon David Thierry,' Rho said when we had recovered. She wiped her eyes. 'Mickey, you're brilliant. But it still doesn't make sense. Why are they so afraid of him?'

I spread my arms. I couldn't come up with an immediate answer.

'The Logologist himself?' William still couldn't grasp the whole of the truth.

Rho sat and put her legs up on the QL stand. She leaned her head back. 'William, could you get my neck, please? I'm going to twist my head off with a muscle cramp if someone doesn't massage me soon.'

William stood behind her and rubbed her neck.

'What are we going to do, Micko?' Rho asked.

'They're afraid of him because they think we can access secrets, truths,' I said, finally articulating what I had known for hours. 'We can look into his memories, his private thoughts. They suppose if we go far enough, we can access what he was thinking when he wrote their great books, when he organized their faith . . .'

'They know he was a fraud,' Rho said. 'They're doing all this because they know they're living a lie. I can't believe how cynical that is.'

'They're managers,' I said. 'They're politicians, shepherds of their flock.'

97

'"Cut the politics",' William said. 'Rho, you've stirred a snake pit.'

'Ice Pit. Frozen snakes. Heaven save us,' she said, and I think she meant it as a genuine request.

'"A prophet is not without honour, save in his own country." Matthew.' William seemed to surprise himself with his own erudition. 'Do you think Fiona Task-Felder wants Thierry disposed of?'

'She may not even know,' I said. 'She's been given orders from Earth. All the puppets are dancing because somebody high in the Church of Logology knew all along where Thierry was, knew that he had had himself frozen by StarTime upon his death. . . . That his cremation was a hoax, not to mention his joining the Ascended Masters as a galaxy-roaming spirit.'

'Then why didn't they outbid me on Earth?' Rho asked. 'Why didn't the Logologists buy StarTime decades ago and bury dead meat?'

'You can't buy what somebody refuses to sell.' I took out my slate and scrolled through a list of names and biographies, from public records and old Triple Financial Disclosure files. Any individual or group on Earth who had invested in Triple enterprises in the late twenty-first and early twenty-second centuries had had to file extensive disclosures with suspicious and reluctant terrestrial authorities. Those had been the bad old days of embargoes and the Split.

StarTime Preservation Society had maintained a wide folio of investments, including investments in the Triple. 'Here's my prime suspect,' I said. 'His name was Frederick Jones. He was director of StarTime from 2097 until his death four years ago. He was a lapsed Logologist. In fact, he had sued the Church for thirty million dollars in 2090. He lost. Did StarTime select its bidders?'

'They could have,' Rho said.

'Jones probably knew that K. D. Thierry was a member of StarTime. He might not have known *where* he was, since he seemed at no particular pains to straighten out the records after the Logologist employees scrambled them. Think of what qualms Jones must have had, protecting the man he most hated from his own church . . .

'To fulfil the contracts with Thierry, Jones's successors locked the Church out of the bidding, allowing only legitimate concerns. Jones had fought them off for decades. I'd say that eventually the Church just gave up. There didn't seem to be any scientific breakthroughs on the horizon. The heads were just frozen meat. No foreseeable threat. New church directors came into power. Memories lapsed. Then they discovered what had happened. It's all supposition, but it makes sense.'

'Pandora came along,' Rho said. 'Pandora of the tulips. What are we going to do, Mickey?'

'Obviously, we're legally required to defend the interests of these corpsicles – but I'm not sure under what law. Earth law and Triple law don't exactly mesh, let alone Earth law and lunar law.'

'What about Robert and Emilia?' Rho asked. 'If we're forced to divest, what happens to *them*?'

The QL thinker interrupted us with a gentle chiming. 'William, a comprehensible stability has returned. All cells are stable at ten to the minus twentieth Kelvin. No energy input is required to maintain stability.'

William stopped his massage. 'Don't think me unconcerned,' he said, 'but this means I can get back to work.'

'I haven't even kept track of what you're doing,' Rho told him sorrowfully.

'No fear,' he said, bending over to kiss her on the forehead. I had never seen William more gentle, more sympathetic with Rho, and I was touched. 'So long as I'm left alone *most* of the time, I'll get my own work done. Save Robert and Emilia. This family is important to me, too.'

I told Thomas about our discovery ten minutes later. He hardly reacted at all – the family meeting was to be that evening, his job was in the balance and he was thinking.

'The family syndics voted full confidence,' Thomas told me over the phone early in the morning. 'They've left this matter entirely in my hands.' He had left his vid off. I interpreted this to mean that he looked too tired, too defeated, to be seen by an underling; his voice confirmed my suspicion. 'I wish to hell they'd kicked me out and taken over, Mickey, but they've got their own work to do at a higher level.'

'That means they have confidence in you,' I said.

'No,' he said slowly. 'Not at all, Mickey. Think. What does it *really* mean?'

I considered for a moment. 'They think Sandoval BM, under your direction, can't do much more damage than we've already done, and the other family syndics will work behind the scenes with the BMs and the council to patch things up.'

'Give Mickey long enough, and he gets the answer,' Thomas said.

'But that doesn't make sense, not entirely,' I said, my voice rising at this sting. 'Why not tell us to just butt out?'

Thomas suddenly switched on his vid. He looked ten years older and exhausted, but his eyes were twin points of fever brightness. 'I didn't tell them about Thierry, Mickey. We're going to try one more thing. You think the president doesn't know why she's been ordered to shut down our project. Well, why don't we tell her? Better yet, Mickey, why don't you play the cocky little bastard and tell her yourself?'

If he had been in the room with me, I might have reached out and hit him. 'You're the bastard,' I said. 'You're a goddamned sanctimonious and cruel old bastard.'

'That's what I want, Mickey: conviction,' he said. 'I'm putting a lot of faith in you. I think this will shock the lunar Logologists into a useful confusion. The leaders of the Church are counting on our not knowing; if we don't know, Fiona and the lunar branch won't know. Let's upset the balance of ignorance.'

I was still angry enough to keep my finger on the cut-off. But his words and his plan started to become clear to me. 'You want me to play the upstart again,' I said.

'You got it, Mickey. Angry. Insulted. I've just fired you. Tell Fiona Task-Felder that we know we have Thierry,

100

and that we're going to debrief his head unless they back off.'

'Thomas, that's . . . a little scary.'

'I think it will knock Fiona into a stupor and give us some much-needed time. You know what the next step is, Mickey?'

'We announce it to the solar system.'

Thomas laughed out loud. 'Damn you to hell, my boy, you're getting the hang of it now. We could set the Logologists back fifty years. "Church seeks to destroy remains of prophet and founder."' His hands ascribed lit headlines. 'I think Sandoval's directors are correct to leave this to us, don't you?'

I felt like a rat in a hole. 'If you say so, Thomas.'

'We have our orders. Sic her, Mickey.'

I waited thirty hours, just to give myself time to think, to feel my way through to some independence from Thomas. I was not at all sure he hadn't broken under this strain. The thought of calling the president, after my last defeat at her hands, was nauseating. I thought of all the poor idiots throughout human history who had been caught in political traps, logistical traps, traps of any kind; all rats in a common hole.

I felt myself growing older. I didn't see it as an improvement.

And who was behind it all? Whom could I blame?

Ultimately, one man who had started a strangely secular church, attracting people good and bad, faithful and cynical, starting an organization too large and too well-financed and organized to simply fade: promulgating a series of lies become sacred truths. How often had that happened in human history, and how many had suffered and died?

I had dipped into records of past prophets during my Earth research. Zarathustra. Jesus. Mohammed. Shabbetai Tzevi, the seventeenth-century Turkish Jew who had claimed to be Messiah, and who in the end had apostatized and become a Moslem. Al Mahdi, who had defeated the British at

101

Khartoum. Joseph Smith, who had read the Word of God from golden tablets with special glasses, and Brigham Young. Dozens of nineteenth and twentieth century founders of radical branches of Christianity and Islam. The nameless, faceless prophet of the Binary Millennium. And all the little ones since, the pretenders whose religions had eventually foundered, the charlatans of small talent, of skewed messages too foul even for human mass consumption. To which rank did Thierry belong?

I swung back from this dark vision, asking myself how much such humans had contributed to human philosophy and order, to civilization. Judaism, Christianity and Islam had ordered and divided the Western world. I myself admired Jesus.

But what I had learned about Thierry made it impossible for me to give him top rank. He had been petty, a philanderer, a malicious prosecutor of those who had fallen from his grace. He had written ridiculous laws to govern the lives of his followers. He had been cruel and intemperate. Eventually, instead of going on a galactic cruise and joining the Ascended Masters, as he had claimed he would do upon 'discorporation', Thierry had been frozen by StarTime Preservation. He had donated his head to the ages, in the hopes of a purely secular immortality.

I visited the Ice Pit and rode the elevator to the chamber. Stolbart and Cailetet-Davis had been recalled, finally, but they had left their equipment in place, since the recall was tentative, pending final disposition of the project.

Rho had been instructed in some of the fundamentals of the instruments. She could play back the recordings already made, and with some effort make crude translations of other patterns.

We sat in the near-silence, squatting on the steel decking. Rho cursed and fumbled her way through the equipment settings.

'I'm going to have to interpret some of this,' Rho said. 'The translations aren't perfect.'

We listened to Kimon Thierry's last few minutes of conscious memory. There were, as yet, no visual translations. The sound that came from the equipment was distorted, human voices barely recognizable.

'*Mr Thierry, a . . .* [crackling whicker] *longtime friend of Mrs Winston . . .*'

'We think he's talking on the phone,' Rho explained.

'*Yes, I know her. What's she want?*'

That was Thierry himself, speaking aloud, heard from within his own head: voice deeper and more resonant.

'*She's asked about the* [something] *logos point meeting in January. Is there going to be an XYZ mind discourse?*'

'*I don't see why not. Who is she? Not another bitch from the Staten Island instrumentality, is she?*'

'*No, sir. She's a platinum contributor. She brought her five children to the Taos Campus Logos in September . . .*'

'Just day-to-day business,' Rho suggested. She rested her chin in her hands, squatting lotus on the floor, elbows on knees, as I remembered her sitting when she was a young girl. She looked at me with a be-patient expression; more coming.

'*Tell her the mind discourse takes a lot of my mental energy. If I'm going to hold an XYZ, we'll need ten new contributors, each at the platinum level. Takes a lot of energy to contact the lost gods.*'

Even through his own filter, Thierry sounded more than just physically tired; he sounded like a man trapped in boredom, mouthing the words with no hope for relief.

'*Can you guarantee contact with them?*'

'*What in hell kind of question is that?*'

'*Sir, I mean, do you have the wherewithal? Your health hasn't been that good recently. The last logos point . . .*'

'*Tell Mrs What's-her-name I'll have her swimming in Delta Wisdom, I'll have the gods evacuate her mental sinuses back to her conception. Tell her whatever she needs to be convinced to work for us. We need ten new platinums. What the hell else have you got?*'

'*I'm sorry to upset you, Mr Thierry, but I'd like this to go well—*'

103

'*I appreciate your concern, but I know what my strength is now. I rest . . . on my own theos charge. What else? Ahhh . . .*'

'*Sir?*' [Distorted.]

A long groan, followed by sharp clatters, other voices in his immediate vicinity, one female voice coming to the fore, '*Kimon, Kimon, what's wrong?*'

No answer from Thierry, just another groan; something like plumbing rattling, fireworks exploding in a muffled room. The same female voice barely audible over Thierry's final memories of a drastically failing body: '*Kimon, what is this—*'

And Thierry's final words, issued in a whispered moan, '*Get Peter.*'

The translation ended and Rho shut off the tape.

We stared at each other without speaking for a moment. 'I can see . . . why some people think this is wrong,' I said quietly. 'I can see maybe why the Logologists on Earth wouldn't want this.'

'It's a real intrusion, not like just opening a diary,' Rho admitted.

'We should seal them off until they can be resurrected,' I said. Rho looked away, at the neat tiers of steel boxes stretching around the curve of the chamber, at the Cailetet and Onnes equipment stacked beside us.

'We have to have courage,' she said. 'And if we're allowed to continue, we have to work out our own ethics. We're the first to do this. It isn't wrong, I think, but it *is* dangerous.'

'Rho, I'm exhausted by this whole thing. We could call Task-Felder and offer to give them Thierry. Let them have what they want.'

'What do you think they'd do?' Rho asked.

I bit my lower lip and shrugged. 'They'd send him back to Earth, probably. Let the directors decide whether he should be . . .'

'Released,' Rho suggested. 'To join the Ascended Masters.'

'He doesn't have any descendants, any family I could discover. . . . Just the Logologists.'

104

'And they don't want him,' Rho said.

'They don't want anybody else to have him,' I said.

She unwound from her lotus and got to her knees, turning off the power on the translator. 'Do you agree with Thomas's plan?'

I didn't move or speak for a moment, not wanting to commit myself. 'We need the time.'

'Mickey, Sandoval has signed for the whole lot, a binding agreement. We have to protect them, keep them, all of them . . . and if there's a way to revive them, we have to do that, too.'

'All right,' I said. 'I don't think I was being serious, anyway.'

'I wish Robert and Emilia had chosen another preservation society,' she said. 'Hell, I wish I'd never heard about StarTime.'

'Amen,' I said.

I hate duplicity. Thomas's plan was the best; at least, I could think of no better. We were being forced to the wall, and desperate measures were necessary, but I didn't like what I was about to do: play the clumsy innocent with Fiona Task-Felder. Smell like meat before the wolf.

Again, I took the shuttle to Port Yin. I did not visit Thomas's offices, however; we had planned things in advance by phone two hours before I left, with contingencies, prevarications, fallbacks.

The first part of the plan was for me to arrive at the office of the president unannounced; defeated and out of a job, straying from the established course of the elders in my family. I mussed my hair, put on a strained look and entered the president's reception area, asking in a halting voice for an audience with Fiona Task-Felder.

The receptionist knew who I was and asked me to take a seat. He did not appear to speak to Fiona or to type anything; I assume she was simply notified there was someone interesting out front and that I was being scanned by hidden camera. I acted my part with some flair, appearing ill-at-ease.

The receptionist turned to me after a moment and said, 'The president will have time to meet with you later this afternoon. Could you be back here by fifteen?'

I said that I could. I lost three hours and returned. This round of the dance was going well; the preliminary steps, the shufflings and determinations of who would lead, who would follow.

I walked the long corridor to the president's inner sanctum. The young women were still shifting files. The replay was hauntingly exact. They smiled at me. I half-heartedly returned their smiles.

The door to the president's office opened, and there sat the fit, blue-eyed Madam President behind her desk, hands folded, prepared to accept surrender and nothing else.

'Please sit,' she said. 'What can I do for you, Mr Sandoval?'

'I'm taking a big risk,' I said. 'You must know that I've been reassigned . . . Fired. But I feel there's still some room for negotiation . . .'

'Negotiation between who?'

'Myself . . . and you,' I said.

'Whom are you representing, Mr Sandoval? Whom do you think I represent? The council, or my binding multiple?'

I smiled weakly. 'That doesn't matter to me, now.'

'It matters to me. If you wish to speak to the president of the council, I'm all ears. If you wish to speak to the Task-Felder BM—'

'I want to talk to you. I need to tell you something . . .'

She lifted her eyes to the ceiling. 'You've screwed up before, Mr Sandoval. Apparently it's cost you dearly. Family BMs are dens of nepotism and incompetence. Do you have your syndics' authorization?'

'No, I don't.'

'It does neither of us any good for you to be here, then.'

'You used me before . . .' I began. Real anger and nervousness added a conviction to my act I could not have faked. 'I'm trying to redeem myself before our syndics, our

106

director, and to give you a chance, some information you might want to know . . .'

She looked me over shrewdly, not unkindly, wolf surveying a highly suspect meal. 'Would you be willing to testify before the council? Tell them whatever you're about to tell me?'

Thomas was right.

'I'd prefer not to . . .'

'I will not listen to you unless you are willing to testify, in open session.'

'Please.'

'That's my requirement, Mickey. It would be best if you consulted with your syndics before you went any further.' She stood to dismiss me.

'All right,' I said. 'I'll let you judge whether you want me to testify.'

'I'll record this as a voluntary meeting, just like the last time you were here.'

'Fine,' I said, caving in disconsolately.

'I'm listening.'

'We've started accessing the patterns, the memories inside the heads,' I said.

She seemed to swallow something bitter. 'I hope all of you know what you're doing,' she said slowly.

'We've discovered something startling, something we didn't expect at all . . .'

'Go on,' she said.

I told her about StarTime's apparent book-keeping errors. I told her about learning the names of the first two unknowns from short-term memory and other areas in the dead but intact brains.

She showed a glimmer of half-fascinated, half-disgusted interest.

'Only a couple of days ago, we learned who the third unknown was.' I swallowed. Drew back before leaping into the abyss. 'He's Kimon Thierry. K. D. Thierry. He joined StarTime.'

Fiona Task-Felder rocked back and forth slowly in her chair. 'You're lying,' she said softly. 'That is the foulest,

107

most ridiculous story I've. . . . It's more than I imagined you were capable of, Mr Sandoval. I am. . . .' She shook her head, genuinely furious, and stood up at her desk. 'Get out of here.'

I laid a slate on her desk. 'I d-don't think you should d-dismiss me,' I said, shaking, stuttering, teeth knocking together. My own contradictory emotions again supported my play-acting. 'I've put together a lot of evidence, and I have recordings of Mr Thierry's . . . last moments.'

She stared at me, at the slate. She sat again but still said nothing.

'I can show you the evidence very quickly,' I said, and I laid out my trail of evidence. The employment of the Logologists, Frederick Jones's suit against the Church, the three unknown members of the group of dead transported from Earth, our triumph in playing back and translating the last memories of each. I thought there might be facts and remembrances clicking, meshing, in her head, but her face betrayed nothing but cold, tightly controlled rage.

'I see nothing conclusive here, Mr Sandoval,' she said when I had finished.

I played her a tape made by Thierry when he'd been alive, in his later years. Then I played the record of his last moments, not just the short-term memories of sounds, but the visual memories, which Rho had clumsily processed and translated at Thomas's request. Faces, oddly inhuman at first, and then fitting a pattern, being recognized; the memories not buffered by the personal mind's own interpreters, raw and immediate and therefore surprisingly crude. The office where he died, his bulky hands on the table, the twitching and shifting of his eyes from point to point in the room, difficult to follow. The fading. The end of the record.

The president looked down at the slate, eyebrows raised, hands tightly clenched on the desktop.

I leaned forward to retrieve the slate. She grabbed it herself, held it shakily in both hands and suddenly threw it across the office. It banged against a foamed rock wall and bounced on the metabolic carpet.

108

'It's not a hoax,' I said. 'We were shocked, as well.'

'Get out,' she said. 'Get the hell out, now.'

I turned to leave, but before I could reach the door, she began to cry. Her shoulders slumped and she buried her face in her hands. I moved towards her to do something, to say I was sorry, but she screamed at me to leave, and I did.

'How did she react?' Thomas asked. I sat in his private quarters, my mind a million miles away, contemplating sins I had never imagined I would feel guilty for. He handed me a glass of terrestrial madeira and I swallowed it neat, then looked over the cube files on his living-room wall.

'She didn't believe me,' I said.

'Then?'

'I convinced her. I played the tape.'

Thomas filled my glass again.

'And?'

I still would not face him.

'Well?'

'She cried,' I said. 'She began to cry.'

Thomas smiled. 'Good. Then?'

I gave him a look of puzzlement and disapproval. 'She wasn't faking it, Thomas. She was devastated.'

'Right. What did she do next?'

'She ordered me out of her office.'

'No set-up for a later meeting?'

I shook my head.

'Sounds like you really knocked a hole in her armour, Mickey.'

'I must have,' I said solemnly.

'Good,' Thomas said. 'I think we've got our extra time. Go home now, Mickey, and get some rest. You've redeemed yourself a hundred times over.'

'I feel like a shit, Thomas.'

'You're an honourable shit, doing only what others do unto you,' Thomas said. He offered his hand to me but I did not accept it. 'This is for your *family*,' he reminded me, eyes flinty.

I could not forget the tears coming, the fierce, shattering anger, the dismay and betrayal.

'Thank you again, Micko,' Thomas said.

'Call me Mickey, please,' I said as I left.

Alienation without must be accompanied by alienation within; that is the law for every social level, even individuals. To harm one's fellows, even one's enemies, harms you, takes away some essential element from your self-respect and self-image. This must be the way it is when fighting a full-fledged war, I told myself, only worse. Gradually, by killing your enemies, you kill your old self. If there is room for a new self, for an extraordinary redevelopment, then you grow and become more mature though sadder. If there is no room, you die inside or go crazy.

Alone in my dry warm water tank, creature comforts aplenty and mind in a state of complete misery, I played my own Shakespearean scene of endless unvoiced soliloquy. I held a party of all my selves and we gathered to argue and fight.

I felt badly for my anger towards Thomas. Still, the anger was inevitable; he had turned me into a weapon and I had been effective and that hurt. I learned the hard way that Fiona Task-Felder was not a heartless monster; she was a human, playing her cards as she thought they must be played, not for reasons of self-aggrandizement, but following orders.

What effect would our news have on her superiors, the directors of the political and secular arms of the Logologist Church?

If Thomas actually leaked the news to the public of the Triple, what would the effect be on millions of faithful Logologists?

Logology was a personal madness expanded by chance and the laws of society into an institution, self-perpetuating, even growing with time. We could eventually tap the experiences, the memories, of the man at the fount of the madness. We could in time disillusion the members, perhaps even destroy the Church.

None of this gave me the least satisfaction.

I longed for the innocence I had known but not been aware of, three months past.

Ten hours after returning from Port Yin, I left my water tank to cross the white line.

We had bought our extra time, and here it was; the Task-Felder arm of Logology was quiet. On the Triple nets, there was nary a murmur from the Earthside forces.

William was jubilant. 'You just missed Rho,' he told me as I entered the laboratory. 'She'll be back in an hour, though. I have it now, Micko. Tomorrow I'll do the trial run. Everything's stable—'

'Did you find out what caused your last problem?'

William pursed his lips as if I'd mentioned something dirty. 'No,' he said. 'I'd just as soon forget it. I can't reproduce the effect now, and the QL is no help.'

'Beware those ghosts,' I said mordantly. 'They come back.'

'You're both so cheerful,' he said. 'You'd think we were all awaiting doomsday. What did Thomas have you do, assassinate somebody?'

'No,' I said. 'Not literally.'

'Well, try to cheer up a little – I'd like to have both of you help me tomorrow.'

'Doing what?' I asked.

'I'll need more than one pair of hands, and I'll also need official witnesses. The record-keepers aren't emotionally satisfying; real human testimony can shake loose more grant money, I suspect, especially if you and Rho are giving the testimony to possible financiers.'

We'll be too controversial to squeeze dust from any financiers, I thought. 'Are we going to market absolute zero?'

'We'll market something new and rare. Never in the history of the universe – until tomorrow – has matter been cooled and tricked to reach a temperature of zero Kelvin. It will make the nets all over the Triple, Mickey. It might even take some of the heat off Sandoval BM, if I may pun. But you know that; why are you being so pessimistic?'

'My apologies, William.'

'Judging from your face, you'd think we've already lost,' he said.

'No. We may have won,' I said.

'Then cheer up a little, if only to give me some breathing room in all this gloom.'

He returned to work; I walked out on the bridge and deliberately stood between the force disorder pumps to punish my body with their fingernail-on-slate sensation of deep displacement.

Rho and I joined William in the Ice Pit laboratory at eight hundred. He assigned Rho to monitoring the pumps, which he ramped to full activity. I sat watch on the refrigerators. There didn't seem to be any practical need for either Rho or me to be there. It soon became obvious we had been invited more to provide company than to help or witness.

William was outwardly calm, inwardly very nervous, which he betrayed by occasional short bursts of mild pique, quickly apologized for and retracted. I didn't mind facing pique; somehow it made me feel better, took my mind off events happening outside the Ice Pit.

We were a strange crew; Rho even more subdued than William, unaffected by the grating of the disorder pumps; I getting progressively drunker and drunker with an uncalled-for sense of separation and relief from our troubles; William making a circuit of all the equipment, ending at the highly polished Cavity containing the cells, mounted on levitation absorbers just beyond the left branch of the bridge.

Far above us, barely visible in the spilled light from the laboratory and the bridge, hung the dark grey vault of the volcanic void, obscured by a debris net.

At nine hundred, William's calm cracked wide open when the QL announced another reverse in the lambda phase, and conditions within the cells that it could not interpret. 'Are they the same conditions as last time?'

112

William asked, fingers of both hands drumming the top surface of the QL.

'The readings and energy requirements are the same,' the QL said. Rho pointed out that the force disorder pumps were showing chaotic fluctuations in their 'draw' from the cells. 'Has that happened before?'

'I've never had the pumps ramped so high before. No, it hasn't happened,' William explained. 'QL, what would happen to our cells if we just turned off the stabilizing energy?'

'I cannot guess,' the QL replied. It flatly refused to answer any similar questions, which irritated William.

'You said something earlier about this possibly reflecting future events in the cells,' I reminded him. 'What did you mean by that?'

'I couldn't think of any other explanation,' William said. 'I still can't. QL won't confirm or deny the possibility.'

'Yes, but what did you *mean*? How could that happen?'

'If we achieved some hitherto unstudied state in the cells, there might be a chronological backwash, something reflected in the past, our now.'

'Sounds pretty speculative to me,' Rho commented.

'It's more than speculative, it's desperate rille dust,' William said. 'Without it, however, I'm completely lost.'

'Have you correlated times between the changes?' Rho asked.

'Yes,' William said, sighing impatiently.

'Okay. Then try changing your scheduled time for achieving zero.'

William looked across the lab at his wife, both eyebrows raised, mouth open, giving his long face a simian appearance. 'What?'

'Reset your machines. Make the zero-moment earlier or later. And don't change it back again.'

William produced his most sardonic, pitying smile. 'Rho, my sweet, you're crazier than I am.'

'Try it,' she said.

He swore but did as she suggested, setting his equipment for five minutes later.

113

The lambda phase reversal ended. Five minutes later, it began again.

'Christ,' he whispered. 'I don't dare touch it now.'

'Better not,' Rho said, smiling. 'What about the previous incident?'

'It was continuous, no lapses,' he said.

'There. You're going to succeed, and this is a prior result, if such a thing is possible in quantum logic.'

'QL?' William queried the thinker.

'Time reverse circumstances are only possible if no message is communicated,' it said. 'You are claiming to receive confirmation of experimental success.'

'But success at what?' William said. 'The message is completely ambiguous. . . . We don't know what our experiment will do to cause this condition in the past.'

'I'm dizzy, having to think with those damned pumps going,' I said.

'Wait'll they're completely tuned to the cells,' William warned, enjoying my discomfort. His grin bared all his teeth. He made final preparations, calling out numbers and settings to us, all superfluously. We echoed just to keep his morale up. From here on, the experiment was automatic, controlled by the QL.

'I think the reversal will end in a few minutes,' William said, standing beside the polished Cavity. 'Call it a quantum hunch.'

A few minutes later, the QL reported yet again the end of reversal. William nodded with mystified satisfaction. 'We're not scientists, Micko,' he said cheerily, 'we're magicians. God help us all.'

The clocks silently counted their numbers. William walked down the bridge and made a final adjustment in the right-hand pump with a small hex wrench. 'Cross your fingers,' he said.

'Is this it?' Rho asked.

'In twenty seconds I'll tune the pumps to the cells, then turn off the magnetic fields . . .'

'Good luck,' Rho said. He turned away from her, turned

back and extended his arms, folding her into them, hugging her tightly. His face shone with enthusiasm; he seemed gleeful, childlike.

I clenched my teeth when he tuned the pumps. The sensation was trebled; my long bones seemed to become flutes piping a shrill, unmelodic quantum tune. Rho closed her eyes and groaned. 'That's atrocious,' she said. 'Makes me want to crap my pants.'

'It's sweet music,' William said, shaking his head as if to rid himself of a fly. 'Here goes.' He beat the seconds with his upheld finger. 'Field ... off.' A tiny green light flashed in the air over the main lab console, the QL's signal.

'Unknown phase reversal. Lambda reversal,' the QL announced.

'God damn it all to hell!' William shrieked, stamping his foot.

Simultaneously with his shout, there came the sound of four additional footstamps above the cavern overhead, precisely as if gigantic upstairs neighbours had jumped on a resonant floor. William held his left foot in the air, astonished by what seemed to be echoes of his anger. His expression had cycled beyond frustration, into something like expectant glee: *Yes, by God, what next?*

Rho's personal slate called for her attention in a thin voice. My own slate chimed; William was not wearing his.

'There is an emergency situation,' our slates announced simultaneously. 'Emergency power reserves are in effect.' The lights dimmed and alarms went off throughout the lab. 'There have been explosions in the generators supplying power to this station.'

Rho looked at me with eyes wide, lips drawn into a line.

The mechanical slate voices announced calmly, in unison, 'There has been apparent damage to components above the Ice Pit void, including heat radiators.' This information came from auto sentries around the station. Every slate in the station – and emergency speaker systems throughout the warrens and alleys – would be repeating the same information.

115

A human voice interrupted them, someone I did not recognize, perhaps the station watch attendant. Somebody was always assigned to observe the sentries, a human behind the machines. 'William, are you all right? Anybody else in there with you?'

'Mickey and I are in here with William. We're fine,' Rhosalind said.

'A shuttle has dropped bombs into the trenches. They've taken out your radiators, William, and all of our generators are damaged. Your pit is drawing a lot more power than normal – I was worried perhaps— '

'It shouldn't be,' William said.

'William says it shouldn't be drawing more power,' Rho informed the anonymous watch attendant.

'But it is,' William continued, turning to look at his instruments.

'Phase down lambda reversal in all cells,' the QL announced.

'—you folks might be injured,' the voice concluded, overlapping.

'We're fine,' I said.

'You'd better get out of there. No way of knowing how much damage the void has sustained, whether— '

'Let's go,' I said, looking up.

Chunks of rock and dust drifted into the overhead net, making it belly in and out like the upside-down bell of a jellyfish.

'Lambda reversal ending in all cells,' the QL said.

'Wait— ' William said.

I stood on the bridge between the Cavity and the disorder pumps. The refrigerators hung motionless in their intricate suspensions. Rho stood in the door to the lab. William stood beside the Cavity.

'Zero attained,' the QL announced.

Rho glanced at me, and I started to say something, but my throat caught. The lights dimmed all around.

Distantly, our two slates said, *Time to evacuate . . .*

I turned to leave, stepping between the pumps, and that

saved my life . . . or at any rate made it possible for me to be here, now, in my present condition.

The pump jackets fluoresced green and vanished, revealing spaghetti traceries of wire and cable and egg-shaped parcels. My eyes hurt with the green glare, which seemed to echo in glutinous waves from the walls of the void. I considered the possibility that something had fallen and hit me on the head, making me see things, but I felt no pain, only a sense of being stretched from head to feet. I could not see Rho or William, as I was now facing down the bridge towards the entrance to the Ice Pit. I could not hear them, either. When I tried to swivel round again, parts of my being seemed to separate and rejoin. Instinctively, I stopped moving, waiting for everything to come together again.

It was all I could do to concentrate on one of my hands grasping the bridge railing. The hand shed dark ribbons which curled towards the deck of the bridge. I blinked and felt my eyelids separate and rejoin with each rise and fall. Fear deeper than thought forced me to stop all motion until only my blood and the beat of my heart threatened to sunder me from the inside.

Finally I could stand it no more. I slowly turned in the deepening quiet, hearing only the slide of my shoes on the bridge and the serpent's hiss of my body separating and rejoining as I rotated.

Please do not take my testimony from this point on as having any kind of objective truth. Whatever happened, it affected my senses, if not my mind, in such a way that all objectivity fled.

The Cavity sphere had cracked like an egg. I saw Rho standing between the Cavity and the laboratory, perfectly still, facing slightly to my left as if caught in mid-turn, and she did not look entirely real. The light that reflected from her was not familiar, not completely useful to my eyes, whether because the light had changed or my eyes had changed, I do not know. In addition there came from her – radiated is not the right word, it is deceptive, but perhaps there is no better – a kind of communication of her presence that I had never experienced before, a shedding of skins that *lessened* her as I watched. I think perhaps it was the information that comprised her body, leaching away through a new kind of space that had never existed before: space made crystalline, a superconductor of information. With the shedding of this essence Rho became less substantial, less real. She was dissolving like a piece of sugar in warm water.

I tried to call out her name, but could make no sound. I might have been caught in a vicious gelatin, one that stung me whenever I tried to move. But I could not see myself dissolving, as I saw Rho. I seemed immune at least to that danger.

William stood behind her, becoming more clear as Rho dissipated. He was farther from the Cavity; the effect, whatever it might be, had not worked quite as strongly on him. But he too began to shed this essence, the hidden music that communicates each particle's place and quantum state to other particles, that holds us in one shape and one condition from this moment to the next. I think he was trying to move, to get back inside the laboratory, but he succeeded only in evaporating this essence more rapidly, and he stopped himself, tried instead to reach out for Rho, his face utterly intent, like a child facing down a tiger.

His hand passed through her.

I saw something else flee from my sister at that moment. I apologize in advance for describing this; I do not wish to spread any more or less hope, to offer encouragement to mystical interpretations of our existence, for as I said, what I saw might be a function of hallucination, not objective reality.

But I saw two, then three, versions of my sister standing on the bridge, the third like a cloud maintaining its rough shape, and this cloud-shape managed to move towards me, and touch me with an outstretched limb.

Are you all right, Micko? I heard in my head if not in my ears. *Don't move. Please don't move. You seem to be . . .*

Suddenly I saw myself from her perspective, her experience leaching from her, passing into me, like a taste of her dissipating self in the superconducting medium.

119

The cloud passed through me, carried by some unknown inertia of propagation through the bridge rail and out over the void, where it fell like rain. Was I to fade as well? The other images of Rho and William had become mere blurs against the laboratory, which was itself blurring, casting away fluid tendrils.

Oddly, the Cavity containing the copper samples – I assumed they were the cause of this, their new condition, announced by the QL, *zero* Kelvin – seemed more solid and stable than anything else, despite the fine cracks across its surface.

Because of my position between the disorder pumps – and I repeat, this is only my speculation – I seemed to have suffered as much dissolution as I was due, whereas everything else became even less real, less material.

The bridge slumped, stretching beneath my weight as if I stood on a sheet of rubber. I performed some gymnastics and caught the rails with both hands. I could not stop the plunge downwards, however. I was dropping towards the lower structure built to hold the heads. I tried to climb but could not gain purchase with my feet.

My descent continued until the bridge and my legs actually passed through the ceiling of the lower chamber. A sharp pain shoved like a spear through both limbs, gouging through my bones into my hips. Looking up for some new handhold, some way of stopping my fall, I saw the laboratory rotating loosely at the centre of the void, shedding vapours. Rho and William I could not see at all.

A sensation of deep cold surrounded me, then faded. The refrigerators fell silently all around me, passing through the chamber and casting up slow ripples of some cold blue liquid that had filled the bottom of the pit. The liquid washed over me.

I describe the rest knowing perfectly well it cannot be anything more than delirium.

How is it that instinct can be aware of dangers from a situation no human being could ever have faced before? I felt a terrified loathing of that wash of unknown liquid, abhorrence so strong I crushed the bridge railing between my hands like thin aluminium. Yet I knew that it was not liquefied gas from the refrigerators; *I was not afraid of being frozen.*

My feet pulled up from the mire and I hooked one on to a stanchion, lifting myself perhaps a metre higher. Still, I was not out of that turbulent pool, and it seeped into me.

I began to fill with sensations, remembrances not my own. Memories from the dead.

From the heads, four hundred and ten of them, leaking their patterns and memories across a transformed and crystalline spacetime, the information slumping into a thick lake not of matter, not of anything anyone had ever experienced before, like an essence or a cold brew.

I carry some of these memories with me still. In most cases, I do not know who or what they might come from, but I see things, hear voices, remember scenes on Earth that I could not possibly know. I have never sought verification, for the same reasons I have never told this story until now – because if I am a chalice of such memories, they have changed *me*, replacing some parts of my own memories shed in the first few instants of the Quiet, and I do not wish that confirmed.

There is one memory in particular, the most disturbing, I think, that I must record, even though it is not verifiable. It must have come from Kimon Thierry himself. It has a particular flavour that matches the translated voices and visual memories I played for Fiona Task-Felder. I believe that in this terrible pond, the last thoughts of his dying moment permeated me. I loathe this memory: I loathe *him*.

To suspect, even deeply believe, in the duplicity and the malice and the greed – in the evil – of others is one thing. To know it for a fact is something no human being should ever have to face.

Kimon Thierry's last thoughts were not of the glorious journey awaiting him, the translation to a higher being. He was terrified of retribution. In his last moment before oblivion, he knew he had constructed a lie, knew that he had convinced hundreds of thousands of others of this lie, had limited their individual growth and freedom, and he feared going to the hell he had been taught about in Sunday school . . .

He feared another level of lie, created by past liars to punish their enemies and justify their own petty existences.

The memory ends abruptly with, I suppose, his death, the end of all recorded memories, all physical transformations. Of that I am left with no impressions whatsoever.

I rose above this hideous pool by climbing up the stanchions, finding the bars stronger the farther from the Cavity they had initially been, stronger but losing their strength and shape rapidly. I scrambled like an insect, mindless with terror, and somehow I climbed the twenty metres to the lip of the doorway in complete silence.

Perhaps three minutes had elapsed since the bombing, if time had any function in the Ice Pit void.

A group of rescuers found me crawling over William's white line. When they tried to go through the door and rescue the others, I told them not to, and because of my condition, they did not need much persuasion.

I had lost the first half-centimetre of skin around my body from the neck down, and all my hair, precisely as if I had been sprayed with supercold gas.

For two months I lay in dreamless suspended sleep in the Yin City Hospital, wrapped in healing liquid, skin cells and muscle cells and bone cells migrating under the guidance of surgical nano machines knitting my surface. I came awake at the end of this time, and fancied myself – with not a hint of fear, as if I had lost all my emotions – still in the Ice Pit, floating in the pool, spreading through the spherical void like water through an eager sponge, dissolving slowly and peacefully in the Quiet.

Thomas came to my room when I had a firmer grasp of who I was and where. He sat by my cradle and smiled like a dead man, eyes glassy, skin pale.

'I didn't do so well, Mickey,' he told me.

'We didn't do so well,' I said in a hoarse whisper, the strongest I could manage. My body felt surrounded by ice cubes. The black ceiling above me seemed to suck all my substance up and out, into space.

'You were the only one who escaped,' Thomas said. 'William and Rho didn't make it.'

I had guessed that much. Still, the confirmation hurt.

Thomas looked down at the cradle and ran his gnarled, pale hand along the suspension frame. 'You're going to recover completely, Mickey. You'll do better than I. I've resigned as director.'

His eyes met mine and his mouth betrayed the presence of an ironic smile, fleeting, small, self-critical. 'The art of politics is the art of avoiding disasters, of managing difficult situations for the benefit of all, even for your enemies, whether they know what's good for them or not. Isn't it, Mickey?'

'Yes,' I croaked.

'What I had you do . . .'

'I did it,' I said.

He acknowledged that much, gave me the gift of that much complicity but no more. 'The word has spread, Mickey. We really hurt them, worse than they know. They hurt themselves.'

'Who dropped the bombs?'

He shook his head. 'It doesn't matter. No evidence, no arrests, no convictions.'

'Didn't somebody see?'

'The first bomb took out the closest surface sentries. Nobody saw. We think it was a low-level shuttle. By the time we were able to get a search team off, it must have been hundreds of klicks away.'

'No arrests . . . what about the president? Who's going to make her pay?'

'We don't know she ordered it, Mickey. Besides, you and I, we really zapped her. She's no longer president.'

'She resigned?'

Thomas shook his head. 'Fiona walked out of an airlock four days after the bombing. She didn't wear a suit.' He rubbed the back of one hand with the fingers of his other hand. 'I think I can take the blame for that.'

'Not just you,' I said.

'All right,' he said, and that was all. He left me to my thoughts, and again and again, I told myself:

William and Rho did not escape.

Only I remember the pool.

Whether they are dead, or simply dissolved in the Ice Pit, floating in that incomprehensible pond or echoing in the space above, I do not know. I do not know whether the heads are somehow less dead than before.

There is the problem of accountability.

In time, I was interrogated to the limits of my endurance, and still there were no prosecutions. The obvious suspicions – that the bombers had acted on orders from Earth, if not from Fiona Task-Felder herself – were never formalized as charges. The binding multiples wished to return to normal, to forget this hideous anomaly.

But Thomas was right. The story made its rounds, and it became legend: of Thierry's having himself harvested and frozen, an obvious apostasy from the faith he had established, and the violent reluctance of his followers to have him return in any form.

In the decades since, that has hurt the faith he founded in ways that even a court case and conviction could not have. The truth is less vigorous a prosecutor than legend. Neither masterful politics nor any number of great lies can stand against legend.

Task-Felder ceased being a Logologist multiple twenty years ago. The majority of members voted to open it to new settlers, of whatever beliefs; their connections with Earth were broken.

I have healed, grown older, worked to set lunar politics aright, married and contributed my own children to the Sandoval family. I suppose I have done my duty to family and

Moon, and have nothing to be ashamed of. I have watched lunar politics and the lunar constitution change and reach a form we can live with, ideal for no one, acceptable to most, strong in times of crisis.

Yet until this record I have never told everything I knew or experienced in that awful time.

Perhaps my time in the Quiet was an internal lie, my own fantasy of justification, my own kind of revenge dreamed in a moment of pain and danger.

I still miss Rho and William. Writing this, I miss them so deeply I put my slate aside and come back to it only after a time of grieving all over. The sorrow never dies; it is merely nacred by time.

No one has ever duplicated William's achievement, leading me to believe that had it not been for the bombs, perhaps he would have failed, as well. Some concatenation of his brilliance, the guidance of the perverse QL and an unexpected failure of equipment, a serendipity that has not been repeated, led to his success, if it can be called such.

On occasion I return to the blocked-off entrance of the Ice Pit. Before I began writing, I went there, passing the stationed sentries, the single human guard – a young girl, born after the events I describe. As director of Sandoval BM, participant in the mystery, I am allowed this freedom.

The area beyond the white line is littered with the deranged and abandoned equipment of dozens of fruitless investigations. I have gone there to pray, to indulge in my own apostasy against rationalism, to hope that my words can reach into the transformed matter and information beyond.

Trying to reconcile my own feeling that I sinned against Fiona Task-Felder, as Thierry had sinned against so many ... I cannot make it sensible.

No one will understand, not even myself, but when I die, I want to be placed in the Ice Pit with my sister and William. God forgive me, even with Thierry, Robert and Emilia, and the rest of the heads ...

In the Quiet.